I0460795

A Talent for Death

BETH DOLGNER

Redglare Press
1270 Caroline St. Suite D120-303
Atlanta, GA 30316
www.redglarepress.com

Copyright © 2016 by Beth Dolgner

Cover art by Shalis Stevens.

All rights reserved. No part of this book may be
reproduced by any means without written permission
from Redglare Press, except for brief quotes embodied
in articles or reviews.

This book is a work of fiction. Names, characters,
places and events are the products of the author's
imagination or are used fictitiously. Any resemblance to
any actual person, living or dead, is purely coincidental.

ISBN: 978-0692723029

For Rebecca and Rachel,
with love from your "Aunt" Beth.

CHAPTER 1

"Another incomplete, Maggie."

Mr. Frasier hadn't even stopped as he walked past Maggie's desk, and Maggie hadn't bothered to look up. She continued to stare down, gazing into the bowl that bubbled with a dark brown liquid. Mr. Frasier's comments to the other students were enough to let Maggie know that all of their bowls held the correct bright red potion.

In this class, incomplete was just another word for failure, and Maggie had been failing all year. She had been put into Naturals classes her freshman year, when students were divided according to their Talents. She had scraped by with a passing grade for three years, but now that they were seniors, the work was too difficult. Maggie had never manifested a Talent. A late bloomer, her parents assured her, but in the meantime, she was a joke among her classmates. She had been put in with the Naturals, assured that anyone, regardless of Talent, could follow a simple list of steps to create potions, ointments and other concoctions.

Anyone but Maggie, at least.

Maggie finally looked up when she heard Mr. Frasier

say, "Oh! Well done, Kody." The rest of the class also turned to look, most of their faces registering surprise.

Even he can do this better than me, Maggie thought, feeling a mix of anger and shame.

Kody looked over at Maggie, his chin-length black hair falling over one of his eyes. "Tough luck, No Talent," he whispered, a grin replacing his usual indifferent gaze.

"Freak." Maggie looked ahead again, purposely avoiding looking down into her bowl. She and Kody had been sitting next to each other in Naturals class for the past two years, as each of them progressively worsened and found themselves shuffled to the back of the classroom, as if their teachers wanted to forget they were even there. If it had been anyone else Maggie was lumped in with, the situation might have formed a sympathetic friendship. Instead, it was Kody, who only ever spoke to her to say something mean. Maggie tried not to care. He was like that with everyone, and she told herself repeatedly that it was just his nature. Still, his teasing was hard to take after completely failing an assignment again.

When the bell rang, Maggie was the first student out the door, even though her desk was in the back. As she rushed past a group of girls, she heard one of them snicker and call out in a singsong voice, "Another incomplete, Maggie." In the hallway, a boy nudged her arm. "You were supposed to make a potion, not poison," he said.

Maggie kept walking, her face fixed on the ground and her books held tightly over her chest, as if they could protect her from the jeering. No one teased her in any of her other classes. In fact, some of the students who picked on her in Naturals were the same ones who had the audacity to ask for her help in math and history. Maggie took a deep breath, willing herself not to cry.

She had started crying once during her sophomore year, when the teasing first began in earnest, and it had only made the other students laugh.

At least it was lunch, and that meant Maggie would get the reassurance she needed from her friends. She headed straight for their usual table, outside the cafeteria on a patio and as far away from the other students as possible. She sat down with her back to the rest of the tables, looking out over the school's herb garden until Bree and Shana arrived. Maggie's best friends were a study in opposites: Bree was short with pale blue eyes and yellow-blonde hair, while Shana was tall with mocha skin and brown eyes.

Shana skipped right over a greeting. "Somebody's down. Naturals again?"

"Stupid potion," Maggie said. "Even Kody got it right."

Bree laughed softly. "Oh, Mags, that's why you're upset. Not because you couldn't make the potion, but because he could."

Maggie pressed her lips together. "That's part of it. It means I'm officially the worst student in that class."

Bree put her arm around Maggie's shoulders and squeezed. "You always were an over-achiever."

Bree and Shana revived Maggie's spirits to the point that Maggie could actually smile when Shana started gushing over her latest crush. "And his lips, they're just so full," she was saying. "Can you imagine what—" Shana's gaze suddenly fixed on a point over Maggie's shoulder, and she shook her head as her hand came up in warning. "Nope, turn around and walk away."

Maggie felt a hand on her shoulder, and she looked around to see Kody standing behind her. "I was just coming to give Maggie my condolences," Kody said. His black eyes had flecks of red and gold, and Maggie felt weighed down by the intensity of his stare. Her mind was still trying to formulate a retort when Shana spoke again.

"Maggie doesn't need you to give her anything." Shana stood, her hand still held up in front of her. Her tray of half-eaten food began to vibrate, clinking against the table until it rose an inch into the air.

"Stop," Maggie said. "Shana, he's not worth getting detention over. Kody, did you really come all the way over here just to pick on me?"

"Actually, no. Come with me, I want to show you something."

Maggie frowned, but at least the tray Shana had been levitating settled back into place with a resigned thump. "Where?" Maggie asked.

Kody pointed with his chin. "In the herb garden."

"Mags…," Bree began warningly.

"I'm not going anywhere with a freak like you," Maggie interrupted, her voice bitter.

"I came to help you, and you're insulting me?" Kody asked. "I can show you what you did wrong with that potion."

"I don't need your help."

"Come with me now, and I won't say a word to you in that class ever again." Maggie was frowning at Kody, but he looked at her steadily, no trace of teasing in his eyes. If there was the slightest chance he was being sincere, then maybe it was worth whatever humiliation he had in store for her now.

Maggie got up warily and followed him. She noticed that Shana and Bree both watched closely as Kody led her into the herb garden. He and Maggie were soon blocked from view by a tall rosemary bush, and Maggie was about to question him again when he stopped and pointed down.

"What? What am I looking at?" she asked.

Kody laughed. "That is what healthy mugwort looks

like. The stuff you threw into your potion was half dead."

Maggie felt her cheeks burn. It was bad enough that Kody had outperformed her today, but now he was actually laughing at her errors. "I don't need your help," Maggie said again.

"Clearly not, because you passed today's assignment with flying colors. Flying brown, bubbling colors." Kody's grin returned and he stepped closer to Maggie. "Besides, I think you are beyond help. You're failing Naturals because you can't even tell the difference between a plant that's alive and one that's dead."

I should have let Shana hurl the tray at him, Maggie thought. She held his gaze, not willing to let him intimidate her. "Don't ever talk to me again," she said. Afraid that she really was going to start crying this time, Maggie turned and walked away without waiting to see Kody's reaction, but she could hear his laughter all the way back to the table.

"Mags," Bree began, "what happened? Are you okay?"

"Can I hit him now?" Shana added.

Maggie just shook her head as she scooped her books off the table, too afraid to speak. She managed to make it all the way to the library and into the little-used reference section before she put her forehead against a row of books and let the tears stream down her face.

It wasn't long before Bree and Shana found her. "When you weren't in the bathroom by the cafeteria, we figured you'd be in here," Bree said as she hugged Maggie. "Don't let Kody get to you. Don't let him win." Maggie could only nod, wishing it were that easy to let go of the shame and frustration.

The rest of the day dragged by, but Maggie was grateful that she had no other classes with Kody. The Naturals students who were also in her last-period history class had moved on to other bits of gossip by then, so she was mercifully ignored.

One of the highlights of every school day was the ninety minutes Maggie had to herself after she got home. She was an only child, and she reveled in the brief period of solitude before her parents got home from work. There was no pressure and no teasing.

Maggie had rushed home after getting off the bus, anxious to be by herself. She had planned to go home and have another cry, but she was so worn out from the day that she fell asleep on the couch. She didn't stir until the sound of her dad's car in the driveway made her wake with a start. She was not looking forward to the inevitable conversation.

"Hi, Maggie, how was school?" her dad asked, sliding out of his blazer the moment he walked through the door.

"Fine. Did you have a good day at work?"

"I've had better. For every change the architect proposed, I had a reason it wouldn't work. We don't know what will work for the new building, but we have definitely built a list of what won't." Maggie's dad was a Reader, a Talent that had manifested itself when he was only ten years old. His strongest ability as a Reader was foresight, and the architectural firm he worked for used his skills to detect future problems with designs: unexpected weak spots that would collapse years in the future were what he usually helped weed out of a design.

Maggie's mom was a Reader, as well, but she was skilled as a medium. She did background checks for government jobs in their town of Telford, Georgia, and the rest of the county. In order to review an applicant's past, she consulted with their dead friends and relatives. She arrived home shortly after her husband, and her lips were set in a thin line. "Maggie, your great-aunt Sarah says you had a bad day," she began.

Maggie sighed. "What does she know? She's been dead for ten years."

"But she is still related to you, and she can sense when one of us is off balance. Now tell us what happened. Was it Naturals again?"

Part of Maggie wanted to reply that it was none of their business, nor was it great-aunt Sarah's, but she found herself pouring out her story. The only part she left out was Kody's additional torment at lunch. Maggie was still mentally kicking herself for having followed him to the herb garden in the first place, and there was no reason to revisit the scene. "It's just not fair," Maggie concluded.

Her parents looked at each other, and Maggie could see the concern on her mom's face. Her dad shook his head almost imperceptibly before he returned his attention to Maggie. "Honey, we've had this conversation. We know how hard it is being teased by the other students, but your Talent will come with time. You're just—"

"A late bloomer," Maggie finished for him. "And you don't know how hard it is, because both of you manifested your Talents before you were even out of elementary school. Both of you are Readers, so why aren't I?"

"You may be. You could have any of the Talents," her mother said.

"Or I could have none of them."

"Now, Maggie, that is extremely rare. Not everyone has the same strength in their given Talent, but nearly all of us have at least some small ability." Her mother's forehead creased, a sure sign that she didn't feel as confident as her words.

"I've got to go study for a math test. Call me when dinner's ready."

"We're here for you, Maggie," her mother called

after her.

Compared to Naturals class, calculus was easy. Maggie had always done well in math: it didn't take any special intuition or ability. Follow the formula correctly, and you'd get the correct answer. So simple, so practical.

Unfortunately, being good at any subject outside the domain of a Talent earned only the barest praise. Magical abilities were what got people the really good jobs. Like her mom had said, Talents weren't given in equal portions. Some people were exceptional in their areas, while others were only mediocre. Naturals probably had it the hardest as kids, because everyone else teased them for having to use "props" like herbs and potions. As adults, though, Naturals became respected healers and spell-workers.

Readers like Maggie's parents were the fortunetellers and psychics who kept the present firmly linked with both the past and the future. Shana was well on her way to being a skilled Manipulator, able to manipulate physical objects with just her mind. When Maggie and her friends were still in middle school, Bree had been horrified when she realized one day that no one could see her, until a teacher applauded her for discovering her Talent as a Physical so early in life. Other Physicals could fly, heal with just a touch, even transport their bodies from one place to another, but Bree always claimed that invisibility was the best. She had once made a bad breakout on her forehead invisible, giving off the impression that her skin was flawless.

If Maggie could have her choice, she wasn't sure whether she would rather be a Physical or a Manipulator. Dreams of flying were nice, but from a practical standpoint, so were visions of doing housework by simply willing the vacuum cleaner to whiz across the carpet by itself.

Instead, Maggie had endured watching all of her

friends and classmates manifest their Talents while hers remained hidden. The only student in her class who came close to being so bad was Kody, but his abilities were harder to define. There were a lot of rumors about Kody, but he himself admitted that he was half-demon. It was exceptionally rare for any human to have either angel or demon blood, and he was the only person Maggie had ever met who did not have pure human parentage. Kody showed only a little aptitude in Naturals classes, but everyone who had been bullied by him over the years agreed that he seemed to have some kind of strange power. There was a presence about him that suggested he was suppressing abilities that lurked just under the surface of his usual complacency.

Maggie looked down at her calculus notes, but her eyes were unfocused as she thought about Kody. As mad as she was, she couldn't imagine being in his place. He didn't hide what he was, so the other students ostracized him for being different. Evil, some called him. Kody's choices had been simple: cave in or fight back. He fought back by always striking the first blow. By the time they all started high school, Kody was notorious as the school bully. That had stopped everyone from picking on him, and now that his reputation was sealed, he was simply ignored for the most part.

I wish everyone would just ignore me, Maggie thought, or that I could be invisible, like Bree. It would make everything so much easier.

Chapter 2

Second period was math, and Maggie knew she had
aced her test. She was the first one to turn it in to the
teacher, and one side of her mouth twitched up in a smile
of satisfaction.

The feeling of accomplishment didn't last long. The
next class was Naturals, and Mr. Frasier walked up to
Maggie as soon as she sat down. "See me after class," he
said. Some of the other students overheard and had to
stifle their giggles. As soon as Mr. Frasier walked away,
the boy in front of Maggie said, "Maybe they're going to
move you to a Readers class, because I'm sure you can
see your future right now." He laughed at his joke and
looked disappointed when Maggie didn't react. Instead,
she turned her head aside, inadvertently meeting Kody's
eyes.

I'm surrounded, Maggie thought. She waited for
Kody to join in or to give her that awful grin, but instead
he kept his face as placid as hers. It was so unnerving
that Maggie finally broke his gaze.

When the bell rang, Maggie stood slowly and let the
rest of the class trickle out before she made her way to

Mr. Frasier's desk. "Sir, you wanted to see me?" she asked.

"Miss Connolly," he began, "I'm concerned about your grades in this class. I know you're trying your best, but I'm afraid it just isn't enough."

Maggie nodded slowly. Where was this going?

"However, I have talked to some of your other teachers, and they tell me that you are outstanding in their classes. I think, Maggie, it may be time for you to transfer to another Talent."

"But I can't do any of the other Talents," Maggie said.

"Which is why I'm recommending that you join a freshman Readers class. You may have better luck reading tea leaves or interpreting Tarot cards."

"A freshman class, sir?" Maggie thought of the boy who had teased her at the beginning of class, unaware of how accurate his taunt really was.

"You'll start tomorrow with Mrs. Simmons in room 214."

Maggie nodded again, too mortified to speak. She was already turning to leave when Mr. Frasier said, "Please understand I'm not trying to be mean, Miss Connolly. You need a passing grade in four Talent classes in order to graduate. If you can't handle a senior Naturals class, then you need to go back to the beginning in some other Talent. I'm sorry, but this is the only way you're going to get your diploma."

Maggie's voice was a whisper. "I understand. Thank you, sir."

The walk to the cafeteria seemed to last for hours, even though Maggie didn't take notice of anything or anyone she passed. What would Bree and Shana say? What would her parents say? Maggie dreaded having to go home and tell them. But the worst, Maggie knew, was the teasing she would get from the other students. The freshman in her new class would surely make fun of her, and the seniors from her Naturals class would make a point of shaming her even more.

Almost all of the outside tables were full by the time Maggie arrived at the cafeteria patio, but she knew Bree and Shana would have already grabbed their accustomed spot. Maggie stopped just before she reached the first table, trying to make sense of what she saw before her. Kody was standing at the far end of the patio, his hands raised in the air. He had shouted something that had made every head turn in his direction, but Maggie hadn't been paying attention to his words. Now, though, she joined everyone else in staring at the half-demon.

Everything suddenly fell silent. No, not silent, Maggie realized. Still. Every head was staring toward Kody, limbs and torsos perfectly frozen in place. Maggie leaned down to look at a student seated nearby, and his eyes had a glazed look, like he was daydreaming.

At the sound of footsteps, Maggie straightened up. "What did you do?" she asked Kody. He was running toward Maggie, a look of shock on his face.

"How are you doing it?" he asked in return.

"I'm not the one doing this. You are."

"No, I mean…wait." Kody crossed his arms. "You told me to never speak to you again."

Maggie huffed out a breath and crossed her arms over her chest, mirroring Kody. "Just tell me."

"It's a demon trick. I stunned them. It doesn't hurt. At least, I don't think it does." Behind Kody, some of the students were moving again, returning to their lunches like nothing had happened. A few looked surprised to see that Kody had moved from one end of the patio to the other, but most just continued eating. Bree and Shana, Maggie noticed, were looking in her direction with concern.

"Why did you do it?" Maggie asked.

"Because of you," Kody said without hesitation. Maggie simply frowned in return, and he continued. "I only figured out I could do this a couple days ago, just by looking at someone and thinking about making them stop moving. It isn't a normal Talent, so I knew it must be demonic. I tried it out on a couple kids, and it worked great. Then I tried it on you. Twice."

"You did this to me? When?"

"I said I tried it on you. Once at lunch yesterday, and today at the start of Naturals. Only it didn't work on you either time. I thought maybe I was just doing it wrong, so I decided to test it on a whole bunch of people at once. It worked on all of them, but still not on you."

This is the most I've ever heard Kody talk, Maggie thought. She almost commented on it, but then she smiled. "So I've finally found my Talent? Resisting magic that others cast at me?"

"I don't think you understand. There are only two kinds of beings who aren't affected by demonic magic: angels and other demons. Which are you?"

"Neither, clearly. In case you hadn't noticed, I suck at everything and don't have any Talent at all. Angels and demons are skilled in all four Talents. At least that's what they say."

"I can do a few things in all four, but no one is going to call what I do 'skilled,'" Kody answered.

"But you're only half-demon."

"And my mom had a Natural put a spell on me when I was little, so that my powers would be limited until I turned eighteen."

Maggie blinked. She had been mentally cheering, all thought of her earlier conversation with Mr. Frasier forgotten. Did guarding oneself against magic fall under Physical? How soon would she be able to start classes in her new Talent? Kody's comment brought her back to the present, and she felt the first stirring of sympathy for him. "A spell? That seems mean."

Kody just shrugged. "She didn't want me to abuse my abilities. She and my dad weren't together long, and she was worried about trying to control me by herself, especially since she's just human. Whenever I complain to her about it, I get a lecture about being responsible. I think the spell is starting to wear off now that I'm almost eighteen because my powers are growing. But this isn't about me; I already know what I am. I'm asking you again: are you an angel or a demon?"

"And I said I'm neither. My parents are both human."

It was clear that Kody wasn't going to accept that as an answer. "Then there is something that your parents haven't told you."

"I finally have a Talent, Kody. Just let me enjoy it, okay?" Maggie sidestepped Kody and walked briskly to Bree and Shana. "You won't believe what just happened!" she said, sitting down. "I have finally manifested a Talent."

After Bree and Shana exclaimed and took turns hugging Maggie, she told them what had happened with Kody. "He's tried it on me three times, and it doesn't work. I can repel magic used against me," she concluded.

"That's so great, Mags," Bree said.

"So it won't work if I try to do this?" Shana reached toward Maggie.

"You won't be able to levitate me, Shana."

After a few moments, Maggie felt her butt lift off the bench. She concentrated, thinking about nothing but repelling Shana's magic, but she only rose farther. Shana stopped as soon as she saw Maggie's face register disappointment. "I don't understand," Maggie said. How could she resist Kody's magic but not Shana's? The only explanation that fit was Kody's suggestion that she had demon or angel blood in her, but if that was true, then it brought up two very serious questions. How was that even possible, and which was she?

Chapter 3

By the time Maggie got home that afternoon, she was doubting Kody's accusation again. Maybe Kody's magic hadn't worked on her because he wasn't as strong as he thought, or maybe her dislike of him made her immune. That second option didn't seem likely, but it still sounded better than having angel or demon blood.

Maggie had a sense of déjà vu as she sat down in the living room with her parents for the second day in a row, preparing to tell them bad news about Naturals. "Mr. Frasier is making me transfer to a freshman Readers class," she said, her gaze never leaving the carpet at her feet.

"We know, honey. Mr. Frasier called yesterday and asked us if we were okay with it." Maggie's mother leaned over and put her hand on Maggie's back.

"You knew?"

"Maggie, it's important that you graduate," her father broke in. "That clearly wasn't going to happen if you continued failing Naturals."

"Richard, please, give Maggie a little more sympathy. It's not her fault that she hasn't manifested a

Talent yet."

Maggie's dad sighed. "I know. You're right." He turned his attention to Maggie again, but his tone was softer this time. "This was the best decision for you. Your mom and I are both Readers, so maybe being in the class will trigger something in you."

"I have a question about that." Maggie wasn't sure how to word the question, but she knew that if she didn't ask now, she would lose her courage. "Talents can be genetic, right? Well, is it possible that we have angels in our ancestry?"

Richard's eyes narrowed. "Why do you ask?"

Maggie briefly described what had happened with Kody at school, and she saw her parents exchange several glances as she talked. But when she was done, her dad simply shook his head. "Your mother and I both come from a long line of humans. Do you realize how rare it is for one of the higher beings to breed with a human? Very few families can make that claim."

"I just thought I'd ask. I figured that's what you'd say." Of course Kody had been wrong. For the first time, Maggie wondered if he had made the story up to upset her. He had seemed so earnest, and genuinely curious, at the time, but maybe he had acted that way on purpose to seem convincing. After all, she had fallen for his offer of "help" after Naturals the day before.

"You have no reason to believe anything someone of his kind says." Maggie's mom waved her hand, as if she was dismissing the idea. "Stay away from people like him."

Maggie nodded in silent agreement, vowing to herself that she wouldn't be so gullible the next time Kody lied to her.

Maggie spent the rest of the night in her room, looking up everything she could about angels and demons. The more she read, the more she was convinced that her parents were telling her the truth about her ancestry. She was also convinced that Kody's mom had done the right thing by limiting his power: even a half-demon could be incredibly powerful, and Maggie hated to think what a bully like Kody would have done to others if he hadn't been restricted.

The next day was Friday, but instead of spending homeroom talking about plans for the weekend, like the other students, Maggie spent the time agonizing over her first class with the freshman Readers. What would they say when she walked in and sat down?

As it turned out, nothing. Maggie briefly introduced herself to Mrs. Simmons, who directed her to a desk in the back left corner. Of course. Maggie took in the classroom while she waited for the rest of the students to settle in. Her Naturals classrooms had always been brightly lit, and the jars of herbs and oils on the shelves were all neatly organized and labeled. It had felt a lot like her science classes, only the beakers and Bunsen burners had been replaced with stone bowls. The room Maggie was in now had a distinctly different feel. The overhead lights were off, and the only illumination came from windows lining one wall. Half a dozen old cupboards and wardrobes stood along the opposite wall, and at least twenty mismatched mirrors were hung above them. Overhead, mobiles showing different constellations turned lazily in the stream of air coming from the vents in the ceiling.

Mrs. Simmons strangely resembled her classroom, her loose clothing and slightly wild brown hair giving the same odd, helter-skelter feeling. Her voice, though, was strong and self-assured. "Today," she began, "we continue our study of the Minor Arcana. If you would please pull out your Tarot decks, I'd like you to find the Knight of Wands."

As the other students pulled silk-wrapped bundles from their bags, Maggie raised her hand tentatively.

"Yes, Maggie? Oh, of course, you need a deck, don't you?" Several of the students turned to see whom Mrs. Simmons was addressing. "Go to the walnut cupboard and select a deck. Let your intuition guide you to the one with the vibrations that best match yours."

Maggie didn't bother to tell Mrs. Simmons that she had zero intuition. I'm sure she already knows, Maggie thought. She walked over to the cupboard Mrs. Simmons had indicated and pulled open the doors. There were about two dozen Tarot decks inside, each wrapped in a piece of silk fabric and tied with a ribbon. Maggie immediately reached for the deck on top of the pile, but before she touched it, she caught sight of one encased in a deep red fabric. It was the most striking color in the cupboard, and Maggie decided that if she couldn't choose by intuition, she could at least choose by what she thought was prettiest.

Back at her desk, Maggie unwrapped the deck and looked at the first few cards. The deck was as lovely as its silk wrapping. It was printed in black and white, with detailed illustrations that looked like engravings from a medieval manuscript. Maggie knew a little about Tarot—her parents had once gotten her a deck in the hopes that she would someday be a Reader—and she began searching for the Knight of Wands. She gasped when she pulled it from the deck. The illustration showed a young man wearing black robes. His black eyes were nearly obscured by hair that hung down in front of them. His arms were crossed over his chest, and there was a wand in his left hand and a sword in his right. The sword dripped black ink.

It's Kody, Maggie thought.

She frowned at the card. Of course it wasn't Kody. She only thought that because of the hair and eyes. They probably all look like that, she told herself. She began flipping through the deck, but none of them had illustrations that looked quite like that figure. But then Maggie reached the Knight of Swords. The illustration was nearly identical to the Knight of Wands, featuring both a sword and a wand, except this time, it was a female figure clad in armor. My figure, Maggie realized. The illustrated woman had an oval face with high cheekbones and wavy hair that hung to her mid-back. Maggie self-consciously reached back and touched her light brown ponytail. Even more than the physical features, it was the ring that made Maggie think of herself. She always wore her grandmother's silver filigree ring on her right index finger. The Knight of Swords wore one just like it.

Maggie blinked and realized she was missing the lecture about the meaning of the Knight of Wands. She pulled her notebook out and started writing as Mrs. Simmons moved on to the Knight of Cups. At least she would not be required to actually read Tarot cards on her first day in class. Maggie took copious notes, though her hand wrote almost subconsciously. Her mind was focused on those two images even as she tried to push them out of her thoughts.

Kody was waiting for her when she got out of class. He was leaning up against the row of lockers opposite the classroom door, and Maggie marched straight up to him. "You lied to me," she said.

"I didn't."

"Yes, you did. My parents said there is no angel or demon blood in our family, and besides, it's really, really rare for that to happen."

Instead of retorting, Kody reached up and grabbed Maggie's upper arms. In one smooth movement, he whirled her around and pushed her up against the lockers. Kody's face was so close to Maggie's that she was suddenly afraid he was going to kiss her. "Stop," she said, turning her face away.

"You don't even know what I'm doing," Kody answered.

"Yes, I do. You're trying to—" Maggie stopped mid-sentence, and she felt her cheeks flush. Of course Kody wasn't trying to kiss her. "I really have no idea," she admitted.

Kody released Maggie's arms and turned to someone walking past. "Hey," he called, putting a hand out to squeeze the boy's shoulder.

The boy stopped and looked at Kody, then reached into his pocket. He pulled out a crumpled five-dollar bill. "Here, take it."

With his free hand, Kody plucked the money out of the boy's fingers and tucked it in his own pocket. When he released the boy's shoulder, the boy shook his head as if he was clearing it, then walked on without another word.

"You just stole his money," Maggie said.

"That's not true. He gave it to me."

Maggie frowned. "Some other demon magic you've figured out?"

Kody smiled, his pride obvious. "It's more complex than making people motionless, but it's an extension of that magic. If I can maintain physical contact, I can get other people to do what I want just by thinking a command."

Maggie shrunk back, pressing herself against the lockers. She was horrified at the idea that Kody had that kind of ability, and suddenly, just standing near him felt threatening. Kody saw her reaction and rolled his eyes. "What are you worried about? I just tried it on you and of course it didn't work."

Instead of relaxing, Maggie felt her body stiffen even more. "Stop doing this to me. You weren't really trying to work magic on me. You just want me to think you were."

Kody's hands came up as if he was going to grab Maggie again, this time out of sheer frustration. Instead, his hands came to rest against the lockers on either side of her. "You are the most stubborn person I have ever met," he said quietly. "Don't you understand? You have no Talent because your parents put a spell on you, too, except you're on even tighter lockdown than me."

"That makes no sense, Kody. Besides, my parents wouldn't lie to me about it. I'm human, and you're just making all of this up to be mean." Maggie elbowed her way past Kody and walked away, wishing she had any Talent at all so she could retaliate somehow.

Maggie didn't even bother going to lunch. She hid inside the library, sneaking bites of the sandwich she had packed. Maggie pulled three books about angels and demons from the shelves and looked through them, hoping vainly that there would be some way to prove that Kody was lying to her.

The information added little to what she knew already. Angels and demons existed on a higher plane, but they had the ability to cross over to the human plane when they wished. Their powerful magic worked on humans, but not on each other. The few humans who had angelic blood often wound up in religious roles, whether by choice or by force, and they were lauded as leaders with better access to God. Of the famous ones who were always on TV shouting about living righteously, Maggie could only think of one who hadn't been embroiled in some kind of scandal. She figured that most of them were a lot more human than they were angelic, making them no better than anyone else.

Maggie had just closed the last book when she saw a

shock of black hair bobbing over the top shelf of the reference section. She hissed Shana's name, and soon her two friends were seated on either side of her.

"We thought you were hiding again, not actually working," Shana said, casually picking up one of the books. She frowned as she read the title out loud. "'Earthly Manifestations of Angelic and Demonic Nature.' Really, Mags, you've got to stop thinking about him."

"I'm trying to prove him wrong."

"He doesn't deserve to have someone as wonderful as you thinking about someone as nasty as him," Bree added.

Maggie sighed. "I don't understand why he's picking on me in the first place. Does he think I'm an easy target because I'm Talentless?"

"Maybe he has a crush on you, but he doesn't know how to express himself." Bree giggled at her joke, then made an expression of disgust. The bell rang just then, sparing Maggie from having to think of a suitably sarcastic retort.

Maggie's last period of the day was World History, another class at which she excelled with very little effort. It was always nice to end her day with a subject that came so easily to her. When the final bell rang, the girl behind Maggie tapped her on the shoulder.

Kayla was a nice girl, and she and Maggie had known each other since freshman year. When Maggie turned around, she saw that Kayla's expression was hesitant, almost afraid. "I have a weird question to ask," she began.

Maggie nodded and gestured for Kayla to continue, and she said, "In my Readers class, we're working on something called transference. It's where you can transfer some of your ability to someone else. I'm telepathic, so it would make you telepathic, too. It's just temporary, but I wondered if I could practice it on you? I mean, since, you know, you would really know if it worked." Kayla blushed, but Maggie smiled to show she wasn't offended. Kayla had never teased her about lacking a Talent, and she wasn't now, though Maggie knew that Kayla's Readers class was an advanced level beyond the normal senior coursework.

"Sure. What do I need to do?"

"Just sit still." Kayla put her hands against Maggie's temples, and Maggie was reminded of Kody's touch earlier in the day. So much magic seemed to involve physical touch.

The bustle of the students around them faded as Maggie's skin turned cold. Kayla's face became a fuzzy blur, and Maggie blinked hard. When her vision refused to refocus, she instead concentrated on her own thoughts, waiting for Kayla's to come through.

A voice broke through Maggie's thoughts, but it wasn't Kayla's. It was a male voice saying, "Tell me you hate me and slap me across the face. Tell me. Damn it!"

Kayla let go of Maggie's face at that moment, and everything shifted back into focus. Maggie gulped in a breath and looked around her, breathing hard.

Kayla smiled, taking Maggie's reaction as a positive response. "It worked, didn't it? You could hear my thoughts in your head?"

"I heard someone else's voice."

Kayla's smile got even wider. "Wow! That means I'm better at this than I thought. I didn't just give you the ability to read between the two of us; I gave you the ability to read someone else's thoughts. Was it someone in here, or was it a thought from before?"

"Before. I didn't even know that could happen."

Kayla waved in an offhand gesture. "It's kind of complicated. It's not like you're reading that person's mind in the past. It's more like their thoughts are already in your head, and you're just now able to process them."

Maggie nodded and mumbled something about Kayla's skill, too distracted by the words she had heard. It had been Kody's voice, and now she knew that he hadn't been lying about trying to use his magic on her earlier. He really had been thinking a command at her, and she had been impervious to his power.

CHAPTER 4

Maggie wandered out of World History without really paying attention to where her feet were taking her. Even though it was only early October, the route from class to where the buses lined up was already something Maggie could walk without thinking. But when she finally pulled her thoughts away from Kayla's transference, she realized that she was walking in the opposite direction from the buses.

I'm heading toward the student parking lot, Maggie realized. Even if she thought Kody was the last person she wanted to see at the moment, her subconscious mind was begging for answers. Kody had a car, so she was heading to the parking lot in hopes of catching him.

Maggie saw Kody walking toward an old black Camaro, and she yelled, "Hey!" When Kody didn't respond, she shouted his name. Kody stopped and turned toward Maggie, one side of his mouth curling up in a smug smile, as if he had been expecting her. Kody opened his car door, and Maggie thought he might just ignore her and drive away, but he threw his backpack in the backseat, shut the door and leaned against it with his arms crossed over his chest. His half smile hadn't changed. If she didn't dislike him so much, Maggie might have thought he looked handsome, with his black leather jacket and faded jeans, and his casual stance giving an air of self-confidence.

"Why would you want me to slap you?" Maggie began. She had intended to sound indignant when she said it, but it came out sounding like the kind of question a child would ask an adult. She was confused and more than a little scared, and now Kody would know it just by the tone of her voice.

"How do you know that's what I was commanding you to do?" Kody challenged, his smile instantly gone.

Maggie briefly described Kayla's transference, and Kody nodded that he understood. "I knew that if any of my magic was going to work on you, it would have to be something you would do on your own. I wouldn't be able to convince you to do something you didn't want to do."

"Like give you my money," Maggie supplied.

"Yeah. And I thought about commanding you to ask me to the homecoming dance, because that would have been funny, but again, if I had any chance of working magic on you, it would have to be a suggestion you might have thought of on your own."

Maggie frowned. "I don't want to slap you."

"Come on, tell me it hasn't crossed your mind before."

"Maybe a few times. You would have deserved it. You've never been nice to me."

"You've never been nice to me."

Maggie was going to retort that Kody was the one who had begun the enmity with her, but she hadn't followed him out here to get in an argument. She went back to the original subject by saying, "You really were trying to work magic on me, and it really didn't work."

And you haven't been lying to me, like I thought, Maggie added silently. She felt like a million questions were flying through her mind simultaneously, her brain desperately anxious to find out the truth.

"Did you come all the way out here to tell me that? Because I already knew."

"I want to know why it didn't work." Maggie put up a hand to stop Kody from speaking. "And I know you say it's because of my blood, but I still don't think that's right. There is something...not right about me, I just don't know what it is."

"Come on. Let's talk about this somewhere else." Kody was looking at something behind Maggie, and she turned to see a group of students huddled by a truck, staring at them and whispering together. "Get in."

"Where are we going?" Maggie recalled her mother's admonition not to hang out with Kody, and yet here she was, trusting him enough to leave school with him.

"Somewhere that no one will be watching us." Kody was already sliding into the driver's seat, and Maggie reluctantly got into the passenger side. She was having second thoughts as she buckled her seatbelt, but it was too late. Kody shot out of the parking spot and careened so close to the students by the truck that Maggie gasped with alarm, thinking he was going to hit one of them. Judging by the looks on their faces, they thought the same thing. By the time Maggie realized that no one was going to die as they were exiting the parking lot, Kody was already accelerating down the two-lane road that led away from town.

Maggie relaxed her grip on the sides of her seat and settled back, turning her head away from Kody to stare out the window. When she had turned sixteen, her parents told her she could have a car when her Naturals grades got better. That had been almost two years ago, and now she was nearly eighteen. The only reason

Maggie knew how to drive—just a little—was because Bree had a car, and she had taken Maggie out onto a dirt road a few times to let her get behind the wheel. As the few buildings and houses on the outskirts of town gave way to acres of woodland interspersed with farms, Maggie sighed. How nice it would be, she thought, to have a car and be able to go anywhere. Kody is so lucky.

Maggie looked over at him, but Kody's eyes were fixed on the road ahead. He tapped his fingers on the steering wheel in a rhythmic pattern and chewed his lip absently, as if he was lost in thought. Maggie felt like he had forgotten she was even in the car with him.

After driving on the same road for fifteen minutes, Kody braked hard and turned right onto a one-lane gravel road. It led through a sunflower field that had grown wild, half-dead stalks towering over the car. The road curved and the field opened into a small clearing with an old cabin at its center. The whitewashed wood structure was topped with a sharply-angled tin roof, and a tall brick chimney stood sentinel over everything.

Kody drove to the back of the cabin and shut off the engine before he finally spoke, answering Maggie's unasked question. "My great-grandfather built it. He died ten years ago, and my grandfather inherited the place."

"You live here?"

Kody snorted derisively. "Of course not. My grandfather keeps the place up, and I come here when I want to be alone."

But you're always alone, Maggie wanted to say.

Kody led the way up onto the broad back porch, where he sank down into a rusting metal chair. He motioned to the chair next to it, and Maggie sat down. "We're not going in?" she asked.

Kody shook his head. "I like it out here better." Kody fell silent again, and Maggie sat back, looking at the view in front of her. The back of the cabin looked over a small pond, and a few geese that hadn't flown south yet floated idly across the water. On the other side of the pond, trees and undergrowth crowded right down to the water's edge. In every other direction, more sunflower fields eventually gave way to woods. It was secluded but peaceful, and Maggie could understand why Kody liked coming here, even though he didn't seem like the peace and quiet type.

The silence between them stretched, and Maggie finally prompted Kody with, "So, about me."

"Your parents are lying to you. You have angel or demon blood, and that's all there is to it."

"I already told you that makes no sense."

"It's the only thing that makes sense." Kody turned toward Maggie, his tone earnest. "You can't manifest a Talent because your parents have your abilities locked down by a spell, but you can still resist my magic."

"If my abilities were cut off by a spell, then I wouldn't be able to resist you," Maggie countered.

"Not necessarily. If a Natural put a spell on you, it would only inhibit the abilities you could consciously use. Repelling demon magic is automatic, a part of you no matter what."

"Like your heartbeat?"

"Exactly. You don't control it. It just is."

"Let's say you're right. Then why would my parents lie to me about it?" That was the one thing Maggie couldn't accept. Her parents loved her and were honest with her. Why would there be an exception as big as this?

"I don't know," Kody said.

"They keep saying I'm going to manifest a Talent any day now. They don't act like they know otherwise. My dad seems so disappointed in me because I don't have a Talent yet."

"Maybe they didn't realize the spell would work so well? Maybe they thought it only applied to your demonic abilities?"

"Or angelic," Maggie added. "What am I saying? I don't even believe you."

"There's one way to find out."

"And that is?"

"We can find a Healer who will reverse any spells on you."

Maggie narrowed her eyes. "Would I get into trouble for it?"

Kody threw an exasperated look at Maggie. "Not if you don't tell anyone. We'd have to be careful about it, though. We don't want to be seen going into a Healer's office or go to one who might talk."

Sneaking off to see a Healer for a condition that may or may not exist seemed foolhardy to Maggie. If her parents somehow found out about it, they would be hurt and disappointed. And now that Maggie had discovered some kind of magic inside her—even if it was just the ability to repel Kody's demonic magic—she was feeling more optimistic. Maybe her Talent was manifesting slowly, and it would develop more over the next few days. With that logic, there was no reason to agree to Kody's proposal. "No, I can't do it," Maggie told him. "I don't want to get in trouble."

"You have to take some risks if you want to find out the truth."

"But I don't believe there is any truth I need to find out."

Kody just shook his head in disbelief. He lapsed into silence again, and he sat back, idly playing with a pocketknife he had picked up off a table next to him. He clearly wasn't in any hurry to leave, even though their conversation was over. Maggie directed her attention to the pond, resolved to wait patiently until Kody was ready to go. She was so absorbed in her thoughts that she didn't stir until she felt Kody's hand on her arm. "Hey, come back from outer space," he was saying.

Maggie blinked. "Sorry. I was just thinking."

"I called your name three times."

"I was thinking really hard."

"Come on, we need to go."

The drive back into town was as silent as the drive out, broken only when Kody asked how to get to Maggie's house, but it somehow felt more comfortable. Kody hadn't teased her once over the hour that they had been together, and Maggie wondered what had brought about such a change. She was still wondering about it when Kody pulled into the parking lot at Blue Fern Park, at the edge of Maggie's neighborhood. "You okay to walk from here?" he asked. "I don't think you want to have to explain to your parents why you're hanging out with me."

Maggie's hand was already pulling open the door when she blurted, "Why are you being so nice to me?"

Kody appraised Maggie for a moment. He opened his mouth to speak, then closed it again. After a long silence, he simply said, "Because I want to be there to say 'I told you so' when I'm right." He revved his engine, and Maggie took that as her cue to get out. She was certain that Kody had been about to say something else. She was also certain that she shouldn't be too quick to trust him. He was still half-demon, and she very much doubted that he had her best interests at heart.

Chapter 5

Readers class on Monday was another note-taking session, and Maggie was beginning to feel comfortable with the new class. Theory was easy enough, even for someone with no Talent. The freshmen were mostly ignoring her, which was as much as she could hope for. She was content sitting in the back, not attracting any attention.

On Tuesday, though, Maggie was forced to raise her hand when Mrs. Simmons asked the class to pull out the Death card. "I'm sorry, but I don't have that card," Maggie said. She had gone through the deck three times, but there was no Death card to be found. The class looked around at her, and several students raised their eyebrows. One girl whispered loudly, "That must be a bad omen!"

"Just go get another deck, Miss Connolly," Mrs. Simmons said. As she walked to the cupboard, Maggie heard the whisper of "bad omen" spreading from one mouth to another. By the time she selected a deck, grabbing the first one on top of the pile, all eyes in the room were on her.

Mrs. Simmons cleared her throat, and the class reluctantly returned their attention to the front of the room. "Death," she said in a matter-of-fact tone, "is not something to be feared. It indicates an ending, but also a new beginning. The end of one phase of life, or one situation, and the beginning of the next."

As Mrs. Simmons continued her lecture, Maggie unwrapped the Tarot deck. It was battered and dirty, and the illustrations were not nearly as intriguing as those in the black and white deck she had been using. The Death card was the very last one, and it depicted a skeleton wearing a frivolous suit and a long red cloak, one bony hand stretched forward.

By Thursday, Maggie had to concede that Death had certainly been the portent of a new beginning: since she had spoken up on Tuesday, the other students were suddenly taking a pointed interest in Maggie. Some kept glancing back at her during class, and a few boldly asked her why she was in freshman Readers. Maggie shrugged off their questions, murmuring excuses about her parents making her try their area of Talent. It was, she told herself, not a complete lie. She simply left out the part about failing Naturals.

It wasn't until the bell rang at the end of Friday's class that Maggie felt a sickening lurch in her stomach. The boy ahead of her had turned around to leer at her, and Maggie knew from his expression that he was going to start teasing her.

"I hear you flunked out of Naturals," he began.

"Where did you hear that?" Maggie began shoving her things into her backpack, anxious to get away.

"My brother was in your class. Is it true that you're a No Talent?" The boy's voice was growing louder, and other students paused to listen. "You've never manifested any Talent at all?"

A couple of girls giggled. Maggie took a deep breath

at the horrible sense of déjà vu. It was happening all over again, with a new set of students. Instead of answering, Maggie swept up her black and white deck of Tarot cards and threw them into her backpack, not bothering to wrap them in their silk covering. As she did so, one card fluttered loose and fell to the ground. It was the Death card that had been missing on Monday. Maggie snatched it up and marched out of class, forcing a stern look onto her face. A final taunt of "No Talent!" followed her out of the door.

For the rest of the day, Maggie weighed what had happened in Readers against everything Kody had suggested to her. If there was even the slightest chance that her Talent was being hindered by a spell, then maybe it was worth going behind her parents' backs to find out. Incurring their anger would have to be easier than enduring another round of torment from her classmates.

When the final bell rang, Maggie moved so quickly that she reached the parking lot before Kody. She stood by his car, feeling awkward and conspicuous. Other students glanced at her with mild curiosity. Maggie was pointedly facing away from the school when she heard Kody speak behind her. "What do you want?"

"I want to try it," Maggie said, turning. "Let's find out if your theory is right."

Kody raised his eyebrows. "What made you come around?"

"I don't want to talk about it."

A knowing smile lifted Kody's lips, not unlike the way the boy in Readers had looked at Maggie. "I guess the freshmen Readers aren't any different than the senior Naturals."

"Did you make them do it?"

Kody barked out a short laugh. "Sadly, no, but I wish I had thought of that. Still, they did a nice job for me, didn't they? Here you are, ready to find out what you really are."

"Just tell me what we need to do."

"I know someone who could do it. She's the Healer who put the spell on me. Actually, she's done it twice. My mom took me back to her when I was ten because she wanted the spell reinforced. She was afraid it would wear off too soon, even though the Healer swore it would hold until I turned eighteen. Her office is downtown, on State Street."

"That's too far for me to walk. I guess I could have Bree give me a ride."

Kody shook his head. "No way. Remember that part about not telling anyone? I'll pick you up, but not at your house."

"Blue Fern Park again?"

"Okay. Let's go tomorrow, in the afternoon. Does four o'clock work for you?"

Maggie agreed, though she knew she would have to come up with a good cover story so her parents wouldn't question her absence. She didn't think the venture would give her any answers, but it would at least rule out Kody's theory. That was, if he turned out to be wrong, and Maggie was still pretty sure he was. She had to admit that his arguments made sense, but she just couldn't believe her parents would hide such a big secret from her.

CHAPTER 6

Maggie could feel her restlessness growing with every hour on Saturday. She was nervous about lying to her parents, anxious about what would happen at the Healer's office, and a little afraid of Kody.

By three o'clock, Maggie had decided that the best way to get out of the house without raising suspicions was to tell a half-truth. She really was going to Blue Fern Park, so she told her mom she was going to take a book there so she could sit under a tree and read. Maggie's mom had assented with, "Have fun and take a house key. Your dad and I might go out for dinner with the Berings."

Maggie carried her worn copy of *Jane Eyre* with her to the park, and true to her word, she really did settle down on a grassy patch beneath an oak tree. She had a hard time concentrating, often going back to reread passages that her eyes saw but her brain didn't process. Eventually, Maggie shut the book with a huff and flopped back on the grass. She stared up at the branches above her, wondering idly what Talent would be the best to have, if she could have a choice. It was a daydream she had been revisiting since she was a child.

Three short honks brought Maggie out of an inner debate about the pros and cons of being a medium—was it possible to keep the dead from communicating at inopportune times, like during a shower? Maggie sat up, knowing it was Kody without even glancing at the street. She grabbed her book, stood, and looked furtively around her before she hustled to Kody's car. She got in quickly, hoping that no one she knew—or that her parents knew—was nearby.

Kody responded to Maggie's greeting with a barely perceptible nod. After a moment, he said, "You've got money for the Healer, right?"

"Yeah. I hope it's enough."

Kody drove downtown and turned south onto State Street. It was an area of Telford that Maggie never visited. Seedy, her parents called it. Maggie just thought it was kind of sad. The old buildings were sagging and gray, and the people milling around on the sidewalks looked much the same. Many of the old storefronts were boarded up, plastered in peeling "for rent" signs. Kody turned down an alley, pulling into a parking lot behind a three-story brick building. He led her inside, pausing only to look at the directory posted on a wall.

"Who are we going to see?" Maggie asked, looking at the faded sign.

"Her." Kody pointed to the line that read "Helena Waltham, Healer: Spells and Remedies." Her office was listed as being on the third floor.

There was no elevator, so they climbed the stairs, emerging into a narrow hallway that only had two functioning lights. It smelled musty, and Maggie fought the urge to change her mind. She was used to Healers who had crisp, clean offices with nice receptionists and the sharp smell of disinfecting potions. Kody seemed to sense Maggie's hesitation, because he turned and said,

"You're not going to wimp out, are you?"

Maggie thrust her chin out. "Of course not."

Helena Waltham's office was, at least, better than the hallway outside. The waiting area was small but furnished with a low table and a few chairs, and the old magazines stacked on the table were typical of a Healer's office. The lighting was low, but it felt more intentional and less neglected here.

A pull cord hung next to a set of double doors, and Kody gave it a tug. A moment later, one of the doors opened and a short, elderly woman came out. She wore a long black dress, and her gray hair was caught up in a bright purple scarf. About half a dozen gold bangle bracelets marched up her left forearm. "Hello, do you have an appointment? I was about to close early."

"I called you yesterday," Kody said, "about helping my friend."

The woman looked keenly at Maggie. "Removing a spell that you don't even know you have, yes. Well, you have money? You two are just kids."

"I have money," Maggie said, wondering if Helena could hear the fear in her voice.

"You pay up front."

"Yes, ma'am."

"And there may not even be any spell to remove, so you may not feel any different afterward. That's got nothing to do with me. No refunds."

"Okay."

"And if there is a spell, its power won't diminish immediately. It might take a while. So you might walk out of here feeling like the same old thing, but the change will hit you later. Removing a spell takes patience from you and skill from me."

"I understand."

Helena nodded sharply. "Good, good. I'm Healer Waltham. You're Maggie."

Maggie looked sideways at Kody. Had he told Helena her name when he had called? Helena turned to Kody. "And you, Kody Brandt, the demon child. When does your spell wear off?"

Kody had stiffened at being called a demon child, but he answered proudly, "I turn eighteen this month."

"I assume you want me to reverse the spell now."

"It's okay. I don't have long to wait."

Maggie wanted to ask Kody why he would say no to such an offer. If it was so important for her to get any spells removed, then why wasn't it important to Kody? Then again, Maggie thought, he already knew what he was, and he was already able to use some of his magic.

Helena pointed at one of the chairs in the waiting room. "Sit, boy," she said.

"I thought he could go with me?" Maggie asked. Kody was far from her first choice of people she wanted to be in a Healer's room with, but he was better than no one. Helena shook her head as she turned and walked through the double doors. Kody said a sarcastic "good luck" to Maggie as she followed Helena down a short hallway and into another room.

There was a sharp contrast between the waiting room and this one. It looked archaic, but the room was clean and organized, resembling pictures of old herbal pharmacies from the Victorian era. The built-in shelves on every wall were made of a dark wood with ornate carvings. On each shelf, glass bottles stood in an orderly fashion even though they were different shapes and sizes. The contents of each bottle were hand-written in a formal script, and the labels were yellowing. A faded green velvet chaise lounge stood at the center of the room. Helena directed Maggie to the lounge, and she perched anxiously on the edge.

"The demon child thinks you're like him," Helena spoke with her back to Maggie, already pulling bottles down from the shelves.

"He thinks I have angel or demon blood."

"But you don't."

Maggie shrugged, even though Helena couldn't see the gesture. "I think I'm just Talentless." Maggie suddenly sat up straight, her face brightening. "Do you have a spell that makes your Talent manifest?"

Helena gave a short laugh. "If I had something like that, I would now be living on a private island with all the money I had made. Speaking of money, this will be seventy-five dollars."

Maggie balked inwardly at the steep price, but she pulled out her wallet without a word. At least she had the money. She had taken several math-tutoring jobs, hoping to save up gas money for when she got a car. Maggie counted out the seventy-five dollars, and Helena scooped it out of her hands and returned to the table where the bottles she had pulled from the shelves were neatly lined up. Maggie squinted, trying to read the labels, but the only ones she could make out were devil's shoestring and toadflax.

Helena started chanting, her words too quiet for Maggie to hear. Maggie's breathing increased, and she felt a drop of sweat slide down her temple. *I can't believe I'm actually going through with this,* she thought.

When Helena turned to Maggie again, she had a small bowl in one hand and a ceramic chalice in the other. Without any word of explanation, she handed them to Maggie, who took them with shaking hands. Helena rolled a stool over from the corner and sat down opposite Maggie. She continued muttering while she produced a matchstick. She struck it deftly against the side of the bowl, then touched the flame to the pile of ground herbs inside. Gradually, a red glow spread through the herbs, and they sent up a white smoke, like incense.

"Close your eyes and breathe deep," Helena said clearly, then returned to her chanting.

Maggie obeyed, though she nearly choked on her first deep breath. The smoke smelled putrid. As she got acclimated to the smell, she was able to relax and let her lungs fill up without gagging.

After a few minutes, Helena spoke again. "We must cleanse you of the old spell, inside and out. The smoke is covering you, and now we must rid this spell from within. Drink." She tapped the chalice in Maggie's hand.

Maggie's stomach turned at the thought of drinking a concoction made from the same herbs that were burning. If it tasted anything like it smelled, then it was going to be awful. She sucked in a lungful of air, closed her eyes and brought the chalice to her lips. Three quick gulps drained the chalice, but Maggie had to clamp her teeth together and think about anything other than what she had just swallowed as her stomach lurched in protest. As soon as she knew she wasn't going to throw up, she opened her eyes to see Helena nodding with approval. The distinct burn of chili peppers lingered in Maggie's mouth.

"We are done. As I said before, you will not feel any different if there was no spell on you to begin with. And you won't see any immediate changes even if there was a spell on you before. The potion needs some time to work through your system. Here." Helena stuck out her hand, and there was a pack of gum sitting on her palm. Maggie actually smiled as she took a piece, thanking Helena as she did so.

"You're welcome." Helena paused, then added, "And keep an eye on the demon child. When his spell wears off, he is going to be very powerful. What he does with that power will have an effect on very many people."

Maggie didn't know what someone like her was

supposed to do to keep someone like Kody in check.

Helena walked Maggie back to the waiting room, shaking hands with her before turning and disappearing through the double doors. Kody jumped up. "Well?" he asked.

"Well, what? I don't feel any different."

Kody leaned toward Maggie and gave an exaggerated sniff. "But you smell different. What did she do to you? You stink."

Maggie described what Helena had done while she and Kody walked back to his car. Twilight was quickly approaching, the sun already below the buildings on the west side of the parking lot. Kody kept glancing at Maggie, like he expected to see some physical change in her. "Nothing is going to happen," she finally said.

"You want to wait a while? We can go somewhere and see if you change." If Maggie was going to undergo some kind of change as a result of the reverse spellwork, then Kody clearly wanted to be there when it happened.

"I should get home. Can you drop me off at the park?"

"Fine." Kody pulled out of the parking lot slowly, and Maggie soon realized that he was taking a meandering route back to Blue Fern Park, keeping well under the speed limit.

"Your driving was a lot different the last time I rode with you," she challenged.

"Magic can be a delicate thing. I'm trying to keep you safe," Kody replied sardonically.

"Drive as slow as you want, but you're not going to get your 'I told you so' moment."

Maggie watched the scenery as it slowly rolled past. At least they were finally getting close to her neighborhood, and Kody was either going to have to drive in circles or give in and drop her off. Maggie reached back to scratch a sudden itch on her upper back, but the feeling didn't subside. The irritation spread, starting between her shoulder blades and fanning out to either side. I must have been allergic to one of those herbs, Maggie thought, scratching harder. Kody kept a wary eye on her as she contorted to reach the itchy area.

The itch persisted, and Maggie gave up. They drove another block before the itch turned into a strange tingling sensation. Kody made a right-hand turn, and Maggie's skin began to feel hot, as if it was burning. Blue Fern Park was in sight when the burning turned into pain.

Maggie unconsciously grunted as the feeling rapidly increased. It still covered only her upper back, and she reached her hand back to feel the skin there. It didn't feel any hotter than the rest of her, but even her gentle probing increased the pain.

"What is it?" Kody asked.

"It hurts. My back." Maggie doubled over, her back in too much pain to be in contact with the seat. Maggie's eyes were shut tight, and her hands formed into fists. She moaned as the pain increased and tears began to slide from her eyes. Maggie felt like her shoulder blades were on fire and breaking at the same time, and her moaning soon turned into sobs. Vaguely, she could hear Kody shouting at her and feel the car coming to an abrupt halt.

A hand pressed firmly against Maggie's right shoulder, forcing her to sit up. Kody had opened the passenger door, and he leaned over to unbuckle Maggie's seatbelt. Careful to avoid her upper back, Kody worked one arm around Maggie's waist and hauled her out of the car. Maggie tried to help, but her legs refused to work properly. She stumbled, and Kody urged her on a few more feet. "...have to get out of sight," she heard him say, but it sounded distant, like he was shouting at her from a great height. Maggie wasn't sure if she was walking or not, and the dark trees around her were blurry. The pain in her shoulder blades had become all she could think about with any clarity.

When she felt something scratch against her knees, Maggie knew that her legs had given up for good. She didn't know how far she had gotten before falling forward, but she hoped it was out of sight enough for Kody's taste. Something slid against Maggie's face, and her arms lifted voluntarily. My shirt, Maggie thought. Why is he taking off my shirt?

It was the last thought Maggie had before there were two loud cracking sounds, like wooden boards being snapped in half. She cried out one last time before her vision and consciousness failed entirely.

Chapter 7

Maggie reached out and felt for her blanket. She was cold, and she knew she must have kicked her blanket off in her sleep. Instead, her hand closed around something hard and asymmetrical. A rock.

"Welcome back," a voice said. Maggie's eyes slid open, and she saw that she was lying on her stomach underneath a tree. A black hoodie was folded under her head like a pillow. Maggie lay still, wondering at the fact that her pain was gone entirely.

No, not entirely. As she shifted herself into a sitting position, an ache flared in the same place where the pain had been. She felt heavy and sore. "Kody?"

"You okay?" Kody's voice, usually full of bravado, sounded small and scared.

"I think so. What happened?"

"Look for yourself." Kody pointed to something just behind Maggie, using a tiny flashlight on his keychain. Maggie vaguely registered that it was nighttime as she turned her head to the left and caught sight of something dark hovering just behind her. Maggie whipped her head to the other side and saw the same thing on the right.

Wings.

The two wings arched up, their tips on an even line with the top of Maggie's head. Their color was a deep scarlet.

"Are those attached to me?" Maggie asked.

"Yeah." Now that Kody knew Maggie was okay, his usual personality was quickly returning. "I guess this is the part where I get to say I told you so."

Maggie ignored Kody, reaching back with one hand to touch the feathers. Instead of a soft, downy texture, they felt hard. Maggie tapped against one feather with a fingernail, then pushed against it. It flexed slightly under the pressure, and it was smooth to the touch. "It's like plastic," Maggie muttered. "Thin plastic."

Kody reached past Maggie to run a hand over one wing. "No, they're scales. Like on reptiles. Or dragons."

"Dragons aren't real."

"I'm not even sure you're real. I've never heard of a creature with red scales on its wings. Have you?"

Maggie thought hard. During all of her research in the library, she had never read about this. "If I'm not an angel or a demon, then what am I?" When Kody made no answer, she nodded her head resolutely. "We need to go back to the Healer right now. What has she done to me? This can't be right." Maggie felt the first tinge of panic building inside her.

Kody collected his hoodie from the ground. He held it out sheepishly. "Do you want this?"

Maggie's cheeks were the same color as her wings when she remembered he had pulled her shirt off. She had been so distracted by her wings that she had forgotten she was wearing only a bra. Maggie took the hoodie and slid her arms into it backwards, pulling it against her chest. Her back was still bare, but there was nothing she could do about that.

"How did you know I would grow wings?" she

asked.

"Angels and demons have wings. When you started having the pain in your back, I knew they were growing in. I figured you didn't want to ruin your shirt. Oh, here." Kody had tucked the edge of Maggie's shirt into the waistband of his jeans, and now he handed it to her.

Maggie stood, but as soon as she got her feet under her, she stumbled backwards. Kody reached out and grabbed her wrists just before she toppled over. The wings added a lot more weight to Maggie, and she realized she would have to adjust her stance in order to balance herself properly. Now that she was standing, Maggie was able to turn and appreciate the size of her wings. Their tapered bottoms stretched down below her knees.

"How do I move them?" Maggie wondered out loud.

"I guess you just think about it."

Biting her lip in concentration, Maggie envisioned the wings unfolding. They shuddered briefly, then began to slowly open. It created a strange sensation in her upper back as the muscles flexed, but she continued trying. The ends of her wings spread out until they were fully extended. Maggie put her arms straight out to her sides, and the wings extended past the ends of her fingertips. With another conscious effort, the wings refolded behind her back. Maggie looked up at the patch of dark sky that showed through the trees. I'm going to be able to fly, she thought, if I don't start freaking out first.

Maggie barely looked where she was going as she walked back to Kody's car, too busy glancing back at her wings. There were so many questions running through her mind, but Kody posed the most important one at the moment.

"How are we going to fit you inside?"

Luckily, the wings were more flexible than either one

of them would have thought. It took a while, but eventually Maggie was strapped into the passenger side with the ends of her wings curved around the back of the seat.

Kody didn't waste any time on the return to Helena Waltham's office, arriving in only fifteen minutes, even though it felt like fifty to Maggie. They agreed that Maggie should stay in the car rather than risking anyone seeing her, so Kody went into the building by himself. Five minutes later, he came out with a disappointed look on his face.

"Nobody there," he said. "I pounded on the door for ages, but the office is closed."

Maggie huffed out a breath. "But she needs to fix me! There must have been something wrong with her spellwork! What are my parents going to say?"

"Don't worry about them. They're the ones who lied to you in the first place."

"But they'll be furious that I went behind their backs to a Healer! And how am I going to go to school on Monday? This is awful!"

"How is it awful? You're going to find out all kinds of stuff you can do now. You won't be No Talent anymore."

Maggie was shaking her head. "It's a mistake. The Healer must have messed up." Maggie stopped suddenly, her panic turning into anger. "You tricked me into doing this."

"Tricked you?" Kody looked incredulous. "No, I knew there was something different about you. You said you wanted answers, and I'm helping you get them."

"But I don't have answers!" Maggie was nearly shouting in the close confines of the car. Her words came rapidly as the reality of her situation sank in. "Now I have more questions and giant wings that I can't hide from anybody! I'm going to get in trouble and people will think I'm a freak and you tricked me so you could laugh at me like everyone else will."

Kody didn't respond. He just sat, stricken, staring at Maggie with wide eyes. He had turned and pushed himself against the driver's side door when Maggie had started shouting at him, as if he wanted to escape. When Maggie's words turned to tears, Kody only looked more uncomfortable. Finally, he said quietly, "What do you want me to do?"

"Take me home."

Maggie had stopped crying by the time they reached Blue Fern Park. Kody stopped for only a moment before he started driving again. "You can't walk home like that. Tell me how to get to your house."

"But my parents—," Maggie began.

"You have wings sprouting from your back. Do you really think your parents will even care that I'm the one bringing you home?"

Maggie answered with, "Go straight at the stop sign."

When they arrived at her house, Maggie was surprised how dark it was inside until she remembered that her parents had planned to eat out with another couple. She had never been so grateful to have the house to herself.

Maggie climbed out of the car slowly while Kody came around to her side. "Maggie," he began, "um…"

"Don't start. I've got a lot to deal with, and I don't have room to deal with you, too." Kody jumped out of the way as Maggie stalked past him, one of her wings nearly hitting him.

"You still have my hoodie!" Kody shouted at her back.

Maggie didn't even stop walking. In one fluid movement, she slid the hoodie off and tossed it over her head. She didn't want to look at Kody again. Whatever his reasons had been for taking her to the Healer, Maggie was blaming him for her current state and all the trouble that it was going to bring into her life.

Maggie went straight to her room and flopped down on the bed, crying for the third time that day. When she was able to stop and think clearly, one possible solution stood out. She called Bree.

"Mags, what's up?" Bree answered.

"I need your help. Is it possible to make part of me invisible?"

"I can't make anyone else invisible. Only myself. Why?"

Maggie ignored the question. "But at school, Kayla did something called transference where I could use her Talent."

"That only works when there's direct contact. You know, like holding hands." Bree paused. "Mags, what's wrong? You sound upset."

"I can't tell you." Maggie bit her lip. I am not going to cry again, she told herself.

"Are you at home?"

"Yes."

"I'll be there in less than twenty minutes." Bree hung up the phone before Maggie could argue. Despite Kody's insistence on the need for secrecy, Maggie was happy that Bree was on the way. She would, at least, be able to offer her sympathy.

Bree was true to her word, arriving well before twenty minutes had passed, and Maggie steeled herself for Bree's reaction before opening the front door. Bree took it a lot better than Maggie had expected. She stared at Maggie for a long time, then simply said, "Well. I see why you wanted invisibility. Tell me everything."

Maggie poured out her story while Bree interjected as many derogatory comments about Kody as she could. When Maggie finally finished, Bree just hugged Maggie tight. "We'll go see the Healer together and make her fix you. You're right; she must have done something wrong. Or else Kody paid her to purposely do this to you." Bree paused and smiled tentatively. "There is one upside to all of this. These wings are beautiful. Once all of this has settled, you're going to appreciate how amazing you look right now."

Maggie smiled thinly, then shuddered as she felt a strange sensation that made her skin break out in goose bumps. "I can feel that. Bree, are you…petting me?"

"I can't help it. I just wanted to see what they felt like."

"Kody called them scales."

"Okay, I'm putting a rule into place: you're not allowed to mention that jerk, or even think of him, for the rest of the weekend."

"It's kind of hard when I've got two massive reminders of him stuck to my back."

"Just try for me, okay? Now, we've got to keep you in hiding while we try to sort all of this out. Come to my house; you can sneak in through the back door, and I'll tell Mom that you don't want to see anyone. I'll make up a reason, tell her your boyfriend just broke up with you or something."

"Bree, your mother has known me since I was five. She won't believe that for a second."

Bree pursed her lips. "Then I'll tell her that a guy you have a massive crush on said something really mean to you."

"Much more likely."

Maggie donned a tank top before leaving the house, figuring out that she could pull it up over her waist and slide the straps over her shoulders without hindering her wings. She put on a cardigan backwards to hold off the October chill. When they got outside, Bree went through the same process of getting Maggie into her car as Kody had.

As they drove, Maggie sent a text to her mother, saying that she would be staying with Bree. If she could keep out of sight of Bree's mom and little brother, then she would be safe from the inevitable scene for at least another day. They hadn't driven far before Bree said firmly, "Shana needs to know. She can help us."

Maggie agreed instantly and called her, and by the time they pulled into the driveway of Bree's house, Shana was already there, her dad's car parked at the curb. Shana gaped when Maggie stepped out of the car. "Take her around back," Bree ordered.

Shana complied, still silent. It wasn't until Bree had unlocked the back door and led them to her room, looking furtively down the hall the whole time, that Shana finally spoke. "Girl, what have you gotten yourself into?"

Maggie repeated her story, though Bree kept reminding her that she was breaking the rule of not talking about Kody. When Maggie finished, Shana nodded curtly and turned to Bree. "Go get every book your parents own about spells and bring them here. Maggie, you get on the computer and start searching for anything about red wings."

For the next hour and a half, the three girls were nearly silent as they looked for anything that might explain Maggie's new state. All Maggie found online were drawings of winged fantasy characters, either half-naked or dressed in armor that hugged their voluptuous curves. When Maggie finally sighed deeply and rubbed her eyes, Bree spoke up quietly. "There is one more book I can check."

Shana's eyes narrowed. "I'm sensing a 'but.'"

"It's all about curses and dark magic. People aren't even supposed to own books like that, but it's some antique volume that has been passed down through our family. If my Mom realizes I've taken that book, she's going to want to know what's going on."

"Tell her I'm looking up revenge spells to use on this fictional heart-breaker you invented. But assure her that I'm not actually going to use one; I'll just feel better knowing my options." Maggie added in an undertone, "Or maybe I can get revenge on Ko—sorry—that guy I'm not allowed to talk about."

Bree raised an eyebrow, but she disappeared and returned in five minutes, holding a cracked black leather-bound book in one hand and a carton of chocolate ice cream in the other. Three spoons were sticking out of the carton. "Mom says she's sorry that boys are so stupid, and she hopes this makes you feel better."

The ice cream actually did lighten Maggie's spirits a little, but as they approached the end of the book and still found nothing about red wings, scales, or spells that made new body parts grow, Maggie felt her shoulders slump.

"Hang in there, Mags," Shana said. "We'll go see the Healer first thing tomorrow. Right now, you look like you need some sleep."

Maggie glanced ruefully over her shoulder. She would have to learn to like sleeping on her stomach. Bree insisted that Maggie take her bed. As she felt exhaustion overpower her worry, Maggie's wings relaxed until they draped across the width of the bed, their ends extending under the edges of the blanket Bree had put over her. "I'm going to need a bigger bed at home," Maggie mumbled before she fell asleep.

Maggie slept soundly, but she woke up feeling stiff and sore all over. At some point in the night, she had rolled onto her side. She stretched and heard a muffled yelp. "That's my face you're smacking," Shana said groggily, sitting up amid a pile of blankets on the floor and swatting at one of Maggie's wings.

"Oops. Sorry. I'm hazardous with these things."

Bree yawned. "I smell blueberry muffins. I'll bring a plate of them in here, then we can go find that Healer."

Maggie ate quickly, anxious to get going. Getting to the car without being seen proved to be impossible: the next-door neighbor was mowing his lawn, and in the daylight, it would be too easy for someone glancing out of a window to spot Maggie. Bree finally had to hold Maggie by the wrist, her face focused on using transference to make the wings invisible. It was a skill Bree had not quite mastered yet, and patches of red kept popping up behind Maggie. "Just walk fast and act casual," Bree said nervously.

Maggie felt her anxiety growing as they turned onto State Street. Bree held onto her again as they walked to the brick building, letting go as soon as they were safely inside. Maggie sprinted up the stairs, gripping the railing tightly to keep herself from overbalancing and falling backwards. She reached the Healer's door and grabbed the handle, but the door stood firm. Maggie knocked. No one had responded by the time Bree and Shana caught up, and Maggie shouted a hello.

"Oh," Shana said. "Oh, Mags. It's Sunday." She was pointing at a small sign next to the door that listed the office hours. The words "closed Sunday" seemed to mock Maggie.

Maggie leaned her forehead against the door and sighed. She felt tears welling up again, and she took a deep breath, forcing herself to remain calm. "We've got to find her," she said quietly.

"We can see if her home address is in the phone book," Bree suggested.

Maggie nodded, but she didn't move. "Go find one. I'll wait here." Shana stayed with Maggie while Bree ran down the stairs, promising to be back soon.

After a few minutes, Maggie heard Shana take a few steps away. Maggie could feel the tension radiating from her friend, and she knew Shana was staring at her. Without removing her forehead from the door, Maggie said, "What is it?"

"Are you the one doing this?" Shana whispered.

"Huh?" Maggie finally straightened and turned to Shana. The two overhead lights were dimming rhythmically. "It's not me. This building seems kind of worn down. Maybe it's just bad wiring." Or maybe it's not, Maggie added silently. The lights continued to fade and return to full brightness, and as she watched, almost mesmerized, Maggie thought she could hear something each time the lights faded. It was a dull thud, like a distant echo, that seemed more like it was inside her head than outside. Slowly, Maggie reached her hand up to her neck, and put two fingers against the artery there. She felt the blood below, surging in time to her heartbeat. Its rhythm perfectly matched that of the lights.

Maggie was debating whether to confess this to Shana when Bree returned, out of breath but smiling. "There was a phone booth across the street. You hardly even see those anymore! Here, Mags." Bree thrust a piece of paper at Maggie, who barely had time to say thank you before the other girls turned toward the staircase, seemingly as anxious as Maggie was to get some answers.

Helena Waltham lived only a mile from her office, and Maggie gripped Bree's hand tightly as they walked up to the small, neatly-kept house. Shana rang the doorbell, and soon Helena was standing before them, a look of surprise on her face.

"I told you there might not be any spell to undo," were her first words. "Are you really coming to my home, on a Sunday no less, to complain to me?"

"It worked. And I need your help to redo the spell you removed." Maggie's voice was shaking.

"Why? It doesn't look to me like you've turned into a

demon."

"I don't know what I've turned into. Can I please come in?"

Helena's eyes narrowed. "What do you mean that you don't know? You look the same to me."

Maggie looked behind her. A big oak tree shaded the front porch they were standing on, and there was no one on the sidewalk beyond. She nodded briefly to Bree, and she let go of Maggie's hand.

As Maggie's wings reappeared, the Healer's eyes grew large, and her mouth fell open. She was silent as her shocked expression slowly turned to one of horror. "What have I done?" she said, stepping backwards.

"What's wrong with me?" Maggie asked.

Instead of answering, Helena shook her head, her eyes still firmly fixed on Maggie's wings. "No, oh no, what have I done? I thought the demon child was just toying with you. I didn't think...I never thought...forgive me!"

Helena slammed the door in Maggie's face. No matter how hard she knocked or how much she shouted pleas for help through the door, Helena remained silent inside the house. Finally, Maggie had to admit that she would get no answers from her.

It was a silent drive back to Bree's house. She and Shana seemed nervous, but their fears were nothing to Maggie's. Whatever she was, Helena had recognized it, and it had horrified her. Her uttered "forgive me!" played over and over again in Maggie's head. What kind of evil creature could elicit such a reaction? Even Kody warranted no more than a sort of casual dislike from the Healer. What was worse than a demon?

Chapter 8

Maggie could tell that Bree and Shana were still nervous around her, but they continued to reassure her and promised to help track down answers. "In the meantime," Shana said, as they huddled over the reference books again in hopes that they had missed something, "we need to find a way to hide your wings. You have some Talent now, Mags. We need to know what your abilities are and how to control them."

Maggie shrugged. "I don't feel like I have any new abilities."

"I know you were the one making those lights pulse." Shana's tone was matter-of-fact. "A lot of kids find out what their Talent is because it first shows itself during an emotional or stressful event. You were upset about the Healer not being there."

"And of all those angelic evangelists on TV, only one of them has wings," Bree chimed in. "The others must have learned to hide theirs."

"Or they never had any in the first place," Maggie said.

"They must have. Otherwise, how else would people

have believed they were angels to begin with?" Bree frowned, concentrating. "They've found some way to make them invisible, like I made yours invisible earlier. Let's see if you can do it, too."

Bree carefully outlined her method for making herself, or parts of herself, invisible. The concentration and visualization, she explained, were the most important parts. But no matter how hard Maggie tried, no matter how much she inwardly begged for her wings to become transparent, they stubbornly remained visible.

After half an hour of trying, Bree tried a new tack. "Maybe two wings are too much to start with. Try to make your right index finger invisible."

Even that effort yielded no results. Finally, Bree was forced to admit that if Maggie had gained any Talents along with her wings, then invisibility was just not one of them.

Maggie sighed and flopped backwards on the bed. She swore loudly as she landed on her wings. "I just can't get them out of the way," she complained.

"That's it, isn't it? Those televangelists don't have wings in their way," Shana said, comprehension dawning on her face. She got up and moved over to the computer, and she started typing as she continued. "They haven't made their wings invisible; they've made their wings disappear entirely! Otherwise, they wouldn't be able to wear those fancy suits. Bree, when you make yourself invisible, you're still corporeal. Remember that time Tim Farleigh ran into you? I about died laughing when he couldn't figure out what was going on. Anyway, Mags, we need to find out how to remove your wings entirely. Here!"

Shana leaned back and pointed at the computer screen. A video began playing that showed televangelist Colin Buchanan, who had given himself the ridiculous title of "Holy and Angelic Reverend Father," preaching to a huge audience. "Do you believe? Do you have faith?" he was shouting into his headset microphone. "How can you deny the existence of God when you have proof like this?" Buchanan stripped off his suit coat and his button-down shirt. He muttered a few words, and his wings sprang out from his back, ripping through the fabric of his undershirt. The white feathers shone brilliantly in the stage lights. "Do you believe now?" Buchanan shouted. The audience responded with a roaring "yes" as they leapt to their feet.

"What did he say just then?" Maggie asked. She had sat up and was now leaning forward from the edge of the bed.

The video ended, and Shana turned up the volume and replayed the video. After watching it five times, Bree said tentatively, "It sounds like Latin. 'Manifestum' is the first word, for sure."

"Latin for 'manifest,'" Shana said. "Who knew that our year of Latin would come in handy someday? That second word starts with an 'a.' Ally? Allay?"

"If the first word is 'manifest,'" said Maggie, "then the second word must mean 'wings.'"

Shana was already typing, looking for a Latin translation. "Alae! Manifestum alae!"

Maggie grimaced. "Great, now I know what to say to make them show up, but we're no closer to knowing how to make them disappear."

"We're much closer," corrected Bree. "Shana, what's the Latin translation for making wings disappear?"

Maggie repeated every word combination that Shana came up with, but it was not until she said, "Oblitus alae" that she felt an uncomfortable tightening between her shoulder blades. Maggie closed her eyes and concentrated on her wings while she carefully repeated the words. Her back muscles contracted again, and Maggie felt like something was pushing through her back into her ribcage. The pain began to subside immediately, and she knew from the two gasps she heard that it had worked. Without opening her eyes, Maggie reached behind herself and felt nothing but open air.

"I can't believe you found the answer on the internet. After all those books we looked through!" She started to laugh, slowly at first, but soon her giggles built to loud gulps punctuated by hiccups. Maggie felt a tear slide down one cheek, and suddenly she was crying, hunched over while Bree and Shana rubbed her back and offered words of comfort.

When the tears had finally run their course, Maggie sniffed loudly and sat up. "I am so relieved," she said.

"Funny, you're not acting like it," Shana said.

"No, I really do feel much better. But this isn't over. We still have to figure out what I am. And I still have to find out what my parents have been hiding from me my whole life."

"Look on the bright side, Mags. You're going to have some Talents now." Bree was smiling cautiously. "Maybe they'll let you back into senior Naturals!"

"And have a class with Kody again? No thanks. I'll take my chances with the freshmen Readers."

Bree clicked her tongue. "You're breaking the rule, Mags! You're not allowed to say his name!"

Two hours later, Bree dropped Maggie off at her house. She was smiling with grateful relief, but seeing her parents was a grim reminder that they were hiding something important from her. Too weary to confront them immediately, Maggie made excuses about having homework to finish and spent the rest of her Sunday in her room, emerging only for dinner.

Bree had admonished Maggie not to talk or think

about Kody, but there was no avoiding him at school on Monday. He found her after homeroom, as Maggie was getting books out of her locker.

"Where are they?" he demanded. His expression was a mix of surprise and anger.

Maggie looked at him coolly, weighing her responses. Finally, she simply closed her locker and walked away. Kody followed, demanding answers all the way until Maggie reached her classroom door. She disappeared inside, leaving Kody fuming in the hallway.

Readers class that day was the best Talents class Maggie had ever been in. The teacher showed them a basic Tarot spread and asked them to interpret its meaning. Maggie turned in her paper before anyone else. The teacher glanced at it, then smiled. "Excellent work, Miss Connolly," she said. Maggie didn't know if she would finally have some Talent at Reading, or if her new situation—while still mystifying—was simply giving her a boost of self-confidence. Whatever she was, she no longer felt like a No Talent, even if her abilities were only at a freshman level.

Kody found Maggie again at lunch, boldly sitting down next to her at the table. He clearly didn't want to allude to Maggie's wings in front of Bree and Shana, and he simply said, "So?"

Maggie just kept eating her sandwich, forcing herself not to say anything spiteful to him.

"Maggie!" Kody grabbed Maggie's arm, and before she could react, Kody wrenched his hand away with a gasp. He stared at Maggie for a long moment before getting up and walking away.

"What did you do to him?" Bree asked.

Maggie shrugged. "I didn't do anything. But if I had, a little pain would be no less than he deserves."

Bree nodded, but Shana looked thoughtful. "Watch yourself with him. Don't forget what he is. Once he turns eighteen, he might want a little payback."

"Payback? I'm ignoring him because he's the one who got me into this mess!"

Shana raised her hands defensively. "I know that, but we're talking about Kody Brandt here. Do you think he cares who started it? I'm not suggesting that you become best friends with him or anything, just that you tread lightly around him."

Maggie conceded that Shana had a valid concern, but she continued to ignore Kody all week. He kept approaching her until Thursday, when he finally gave up, but he never again tried to touch Maggie.

As the week had gone on, Maggie became more and more concerned about not having any answers, and she was dreading the inevitable conversation with her parents. By Friday, she was so lost in her world of "what if?" that, for the first time since the previous Saturday, she was able to completely push thoughts about Kody out of her mind. It wasn't until she heard his name during her final class on Friday, World History, that she remembered him.

"I don't know how it happened!" The bewildered whisper came from Alexia Maynard, one of the most popular girls in the senior class, who was leaning over to talk to her best friend. "He walked up to me, and I just blurted out the question! I had wanted to go to homecoming by myself, so I could dance with all the guys on the football team."

Maggie had to cover her mouth to suppress a snicker. She knew Kody must have touched Alexia to plant the idea of asking him to the homecoming dance, which was coming up the following night. Maggie didn't know if Kody really liked Alexia or if he had done it just for the feeling of power, but she suspected the latter. It had been a mean thing for him to do, but then, Alexia had been one of the most vocal teasers of Maggie over the past few years, so she didn't feel too sorry for Alexia.

"Still," Alexia was saying now, "maybe it will be kind of cool. He's mysterious, a bad boy."

"He's a freak of nature," her friend retorted.

Maggie felt an unexpected twinge of anger. Just a couple of weeks ago, she had called Kody a freak to his face. Now, she was a freak, too. She suddenly hated the word, and she hated herself a little for having said it to Kody.

I'm a hypocrite, Maggie thought. I complain about how mean people are to me, and then I'm mean to Kody. Maggie shook her head, as if she could clear away the feeling. No, she reminded herself, Kody was the one who had been teasing her, calling her No Talent. She had simply defended herself.

I will not start feeling sorry for him, Maggie told herself firmly.

Maggie was repeating those words like a mantra when she saw Kody after the bell rang. He was standing outside her classroom, and even though she assumed he was there to see her, he was actually waiting for Alexia. As he greeted Alexia with a smug smile and turned to walk with her, Maggie saw that the girls around them looked horrified, while the boys all looked jealous, even offended. Maggie wouldn't be surprised if a few of them came looking for a fight before the end of the homecoming dance on Saturday.

CHAPTER 9

Bree and Shana both had dates for homecoming. They had tried to get Maggie to go, too, but she adamantly refused every time they proposed the plan. She would have felt like a fifth wheel with them and their dates, and she could already imagine what her former Naturals classmates would say if the girl with no Talent showed up stag for a dance.

While her best friends were preparing for the dance on Saturday, Maggie walked to Blue Fern Park, this time clutching a copy of *Wuthering Heights*. Halloween was just a week away, and Maggie was wearing a light sweater even though the sun was shining.

Going to the park was, Maggie knew, just another excuse to delay talking to her parents. She lay down on a grassy spot that was enclosed by overgrown holly bushes on three sides, providing a secluded area. Instead of reading, Maggie sat with her legs stretched out in front of her and began trying various Talents. She tried to levitate a fallen leaf, and she attempted to turn a blade of grass blue. When both of those failed, she lay back and looked at the sky, wondering if she would be able to

Read the shapes of the clouds. Some people swore you could see your future in the sky above.

There were only a few clouds in the sky, and they moved lazily past. A mockingbird broke out in song from a nearby tree, and Maggie's eyelids began to close. She dozed lightly, not stirring until a footstep close to her ear brought her into anxious wakefulness. She opened her eyes to see Kody standing over her, his face upside down from her perspective.

Maggie stood up, uncomfortable with the feeling that being on the ground below Kody gave him the advantage. She was going to ignore him again, just as she had all week, when she blurted out, "Shouldn't you be getting ready for the dance?"

Kody paused, obviously surprised by her line of questioning. After a moment, he said sarcastically, "Yeah, I might be late for my hair appointment."

When Maggie didn't respond, he looked at the ground and said quietly, "My birthday is tomorrow."

"And?"

"I expect the spell will lift at midnight tonight. I want you to be with me when it happens."

"You're going to the dance with Alexia tonight."

"Are you jealous?" Kody looked up at her, a small smile on his lips. Maggie couldn't tell if he was joking.

"Definitely not." The words sounded harsher than she had intended. "I'm just saying that I don't know how you expect me to come out and celebrate your birthday when you're going to be with her all evening. She and I aren't exactly friends."

"I'll take her home before midnight. I doubt she'll stay with me for that long, anyway." Kody looked expectantly at Maggie. "So you'll come with me tonight?"

"No. The last time I did something with you, I wound up with wings and a whole lot of questions, remember?

Why would I want to come to your birthday party, or whatever you're planning?"

Kody was looking at the ground again. "Because you've been through it already. You know what it will be like."

Maggie took a step back as she realized why Kody had been so anxious to take her to the Healer. "You did trick me into getting my spell removed! You wanted to see what it would be like for someone else to go through it before it would be your turn."

Kody shrugged noncommittally.

At least a dozen words ran through Maggie's mind, words that she wanted to shout at him. Selfish and dishonest were the ones that rose to the top. Her hands balled into fists, and Maggie squeezed her eyes shut to block him from her view. She opened her mouth to speak, but she knew she would start shouting.

When Maggie opened her eyes again, Kody was already walking away. He didn't need to hear her answer to know that it would be another refusal.

Maggie walked home slowly, her mood darkened by the encounter with Kody. It was more than just feeling angry at him; she felt betrayed. It was foolish, she knew. Kody had never been her friend, and she had certainly never had a reason to trust him. Still, she was disappointed to know his true reason for taking her to the healer. It felt more personal than his usual bullying behavior, and Maggie chided herself for feeling so hurt by someone like him.

Although she had refused to go to the homecoming dance, Bree and Shana had finally coerced Maggie into agreeing to a sleepover at Shana's house afterward. Maggie figured it might be fun to hear all of the gossip from the dance, even though she felt a bitter twang when she thought of everyone being there except her.

The dance would go until ten, so Maggie wasn't

planning to arrive at Shana's until 10:30. After a long evening, spent mostly in her room, Maggie and her mom climbed in the car for the short drive.

"Mom," Maggie began as soon as they had pulled out of the driveway.

"Yes, dear?" Wendy Connolly had soft features and, usually, a smile on her face. But as she glanced toward Maggie, there was a tinge of worry in her expression.

There was a pause as Maggie tried to form the words, "Why did you lie to me about what I am?" Her lips seemed frozen in place.

"Maggie?" her mom prompted as the silence stretched.

"Did I tell you about Readers class on Friday? The teacher was really happy with my Tarot work." Maggie chided herself for changing tack, but she had been unable to muster the courage she needed to question her mother.

Wendy's face relaxed slightly, and the smile that Maggie was so used to returned. "That's really great, honey. I'm so glad that changing classes is proving to be a positive experience."

"Yeah."

The rest of the drive passed with small talk, and Maggie got out of the car at Shana's house in an even worse mood than she had been in after her earlier encounter with Kody. She forced a pleasant expression onto her face for Shana's mom, who opened the door and gave her a warm hug. "They just got changed out of their dresses. Go on back," she said.

Maggie was a little disappointed that she didn't get to see her friends in their homecoming dresses, but she giggled at the sight of them in their pajamas, their hair and makeup still intact. Just being with them, Maggie knew, would help improve her state of mind. She continued feeling that way as Shana launched into a blow-by-blow account of the homecoming queen's disastrous attempt to dance in too-high heels, and as Bree described Mr. Frasier's 70s-era ruffled shirt.

But as much as Maggie wanted to keep laughing with them about all of the silly things that had happened, her curiosity got the best of her. "So how were Kody and Alexia?"

Bree and Shana shared a knowing look. "They lasted about five minutes," Bree said. "Alexia looked radiant when they walked in, but as soon as he let go of her hand, she was off to hang out with the popular gang."

So Kody had continued using his persuasion on Alexia. Maggie wondered what that had been like for her, bouncing between regret and joy, depending on whether or not she was in physical contact with Kody.

"He asked about you," Shana said quietly. "I think he actually wanted to see you."

Maggie sniffed derisively. "So he could make fun of me, no doubt."

"Well, he didn't stick around for long after that. I'm not even sure how Alexia got home." Shana made a face of mock worry.

"I'm sure someone on the football team volunteered," Maggie said. She hesitated, then told them about her conversation with Kody earlier that day, his wish to begin his birthday with her, and his admission of why he had talked her into going to the Healer.

"Jerk," Shana muttered when Maggie finished her story. She punched the air. "If he comes near you again, I'll hit him. Or throw the largest thing I can levitate at him."

Bree was silent, chewing her lip thoughtfully. Shana poked her arm, "Hey, aren't you going to be indignant on behalf of Mags?"

But Bree just sighed and chewed her lip thoughtfully. "Mags, tricking you and pretending that he wanted to help you was mean. But even he admitted that he wanted to see what he was going to have to endure on his birthday. Don't you see? He's terrified."

"He should be. Sprouting wings hurts like hell."

"And he wants you there to help him through it."

"Then he should have tried being nice to me, instead of completely screwing up my life." Maggie smiled reluctantly and waved a teasing finger at Bree. "First Shana was telling me not to ignore him, and now you actually want me to be nice to him!"

"Maggie, I know you don't want to hear this, but," Bree took a breath, then continued on in a rush, as if she was afraid of being interrupted, "he helped you when your spell was removed. He stayed with you after you passed out, and he got you home. He could just as easily have walked away."

"It was his fault I had the spell removed in the first place!" Maggie protested.

"I know that, but after he saw the pain you went through, he knew what he was up against. He got the information he wanted, but he stayed, anyway."

Maggie dropped her head into her hands, all levity gone. "You think I should return the favor."

Shana, who had been observing the exchange between Maggie and Bree like someone watching a tennis match, finally spoke up. "You don't have to do anything you don't want to do."

Maggie looked up, but although she was looking at Shana, she was picturing the look she had seen on Kody's face in the park and hearing the quiet, pleading tone of his voice. "I've been unfair to him," Maggie finally said. "He did help me after the spell was lifted, and then afterwards, I never gave him the chance to apologize or anything. I just ignored him. Not that he would have apologized, but still." Maggie put her head in her hands again. "Great, not only am I an unidentified creature, but I'm a total bitch of an unidentified creature."

"So make amends by going to find him. You've got twenty-nine minutes until midnight." Bree was already reaching out to help Maggie to her feet.

"I don't know where to find him. He didn't say where he would be."

"Can you think of where a guy might go when he's about to go through an immensely painful, very personal transformation?" Shana was looking at Maggie like her Naturals teachers used to, when they thought she should already know the answers to her questions.

"Maybe he's at home." The answer struck Maggie, and she turned to Bree. "I need your car, quick!"

"You don't have your license!" Bree looked torn between dismay and excitement.

"I'll be careful, I promise. You've taught me how to drive, and there won't be many other cars on the road at this hour."

"If you crash my car, I won't tell you about the prank the yearbook staff pulled at the dance." Bree held out her keys. "Be careful."

"And climb out my window," Shana added. "You don't want my parents to see you taking off like this."

Maggie was already opening the window before Shana finished her sentence. She climbed over the ledge and deftly stepped across a flowerbed, then sprinted to Bree's car. Since it was parked on the street instead of in the driveway, Maggie hoped that Shana's parents wouldn't notice the sound of the engine turning over.

Maggie glanced at the clock on the dashboard: 11:34. She eased the car into motion, forcing herself to drive carefully despite her anxiety. As Maggie had predicted, there was little traffic. Even the school looked deserted, the students long since gone home or on to a party somewhere. The scrolling marquee outside the school flashed the words "Homecoming Dance Tonight!" followed by the current time of 11:43. Maggie sped up.

The clock read 11:58 when Maggie finally slowed, looking for the dirt road that led to Kody's grandfather's cabin. By the time she saw it and turned, another minute had ticked by. Maggie drove as quickly as she dared down the narrow dirt road, her arms shaking with adrenaline. In her race against the clock, she had completely forgotten about her reluctance to even see Kody, let alone help him.

The road curved to the left, and ahead of her, Maggie saw Kody's Camaro. She braked and the car jerked to a stop. Maggie put it into park and jumped out, not bothering to turn the car off or to shut the door behind her. She ran toward the back porch, but before she got there, she spotted Kody standing a few yards away from the pond. Maggie shifted direction and headed for him, his silhouette standing out against the rest of the landscape. As she drew near, she could see that Kody was still wearing his tuxedo. He slipped the jacket off and laid it on the ground next to him. He was unbuttoning his black shirt when Maggie reached him. She said his name, and Kody looked up, a surprised expression on his face. In his concentration, he hadn't even heard Maggie arrive. "You came," he said.

Maggie nodded. "Has it started yet?"

"No." Kody slid his shirt off and laid it on top of his jacket. He inhaled sharply. "Yes."

Although Maggie's wings had first made their presence known with an itching sensation, Kody was in instant pain. His face contorted, and even in the dim light from the stars and the car's headlights, Maggie could see his body begin to shake. Kody cried out once, then fell to his knees. On instinct, Maggie dropped to her own in front of him, her hands reaching out but not quite touching Kody's skin. She was suddenly afraid to make contact with him, and a little embarrassed about grasping his bare shoulders.

Kody moaned, and pity welled up inside Maggie. Her mantra from earlier in the week floated into her mind, "I will not feel sorry for him." But however dishonest Kody had been with her, she could sympathize with the torture he was undergoing now.

There was a loud crack, like Maggie had heard during her own transformation. A second one quickly followed. Kody moaned again and leaned forward until his forehead came to rest on Maggie's thighs. Maggie watched, horrified yet fascinated, as two dark lines appeared down Kody's back, running parallel to his spine. The lines began to push outward, growing away from the skin. Kody started to yell, his voice muffled against Maggie's legs.

With a sound like ripping paper, Kody's wings made one last push out of his flesh until they rose, whole and unhindered, above his body. They peeled away from each other and floated down until their ends rested on the ground on either side of Kody.

Kody shuddered and fell silent, his deep breaths the only indication that he was still conscious. He sucked in air like someone who had been held underwater. In the ensuing stillness, Maggie realized that Kody's hands were clamped against the sides of her legs, his fingers digging in painfully even through her jeans. Carefully, hesitantly, Maggie reached down and put one hand on Kody's head. Her other reached out to brush the edge of one wing.

Maggie peered at the wings. They looked like batwings, black and sinewy. While hers sprouted from her shoulder blades, Kody's ran nearly the length of his back, from his shoulder blades to his waist. Once he stood up, Maggie doubted that they would be as tall as hers, but they looked like they were wider. As she watched, the wings rose a few inches off the ground and hovered there.

Kody sighed deeply, and Maggie realized with a start that she had been absent-mindedly running her fingers through his hair. "Are you okay?" she asked gently.

Kody turned his head so that his cheek rested on one of Maggie's legs. "That was awful."

"Yeah."

"No wonder you were mad at me."

Maggie had no answer for that, so she remained silent. With a grunt, Kody pushed himself into a sitting position. His hair had fallen down over his face, and he pulled it back with one hand. "How do they look?"

"Big. It's hard to see details in the dark. Try to move them."

A look of concentration came over Kody's face, but after a few moments the wings began to contract. "Ow," he murmured.

"Come on, let's go take a look in the headlights." Maggie stayed close by as Kody rose to his feet, tottering a little with the new weight on his back. He rolled his shoulders back, winced, and walked to the car, the wings brushing the ground behind him.

In the light, the wings looked even more like a bat's. The light shone through the edges, where the taut skin was thinnest, giving them a slight amber glow. Kody slowly lifted them until they were fully extended, stretching wider than the car. "Nice," he said coolly.

"Don't pretend you're not excited," Maggie chided.

Kody reached back and ran his hands along them. "Have you learned to fly yet?"

"No. I haven't even tried."

"Let's come out here after school on Monday and practice."

"Um, okay." Maggie was reminded of Shana's warning, and wondered how safe it would be to come here with Kody now that his powers were unleashed. There would, undoubtedly, be new abilities he was eager to discover and test on unwilling subjects. Then again, Maggie thought, I may not be safe with him right now.

But if Kody had any demonic Talents that the spell had been hiding, he didn't seem interested in finding out at that moment. He looked away from his wings long enough to ask, "How did you hide them?"

Maggie told Kody about their discovery of "manifestum alae" and "oblitus alae." When Kody's wings disappeared on his fourth try, he looked disappointed. "Manifestum alae!" he shouted, and the wings sprang back into place. He smiled. It was, Maggie thought, a sinister look.

"Well," she said, suddenly anxious to leave, "I guess I'd better go. I need to get the car back to Bree before she gets worried."

Kody nodded. "Sure. I'm going to stay here a while."

Maggie had already reached the car door when Kody took a step toward her. "Thanks," he said, averting his eyes.

He was clearly uncomfortable with the word, but Maggie knew he was being sincere. "You're welcome." She began to climb in the car, then stopped as an idea quickly formed. "I still have no idea what I am or what I can do. When you found me at the park today, I was trying to, you know, experiment."

"Really? Because it looked like you were sleeping." The old Kody is still there, Maggie thought, beneath the gratitude.

"Before I fell asleep. Look, my point is, you're going to have new Talents to discover, too. If you want, we can try stuff together. If we're going to learn to fly together, why not try our Talents, too?"

Kody shrugged. "Sure."

As Maggie drove away, going much slower than she

had on the way out, she wondered if she had been wrong to make that proposal. Kody was going to be dangerous, she knew, and he could potentially hurt her, even by accident. But if she was working with him and helping him discover his potential, then she was less likely to be a target. If he thinks I'm on his side, Maggie decided, then I'll be safer than anyone else. She tried to push away the small voice that said she had offered to help not for her own protection, but for his.

CHAPTER 10

As promising as the prospect of flying was, it was also daunting. The entire first week that Maggie had her wings, safely hidden by her spellwork, she had daydreamed in class about soaring above the town, but she had never felt the urge to actually try getting off the ground. With every minute that ticked by on Monday, Maggie felt a growing sense of fear. She regretted agreeing to learn to fly with Kody; if she made any mistakes or got hurt, he was not the person she wanted to be with.

During lunch, Maggie suspected that she might not have to go through with her promise after all. Kody walked right past her, barely glancing in her direction. Maggie even opened her mouth to ask where they should meet after the last bell, but Kody never gave her the chance. It was as if their encounter on Saturday night had never happened. Maggie shrugged, inwardly relieved that she might get to go home to a normal afternoon of homework.

When history class ended, Maggie paused outside the classroom, debating whether to turn toward the buses or toward the student parking lot. Finally, she turned toward the buses. She soothed her guilt by telling herself that Kody's behavior at lunch clearly indicated that their plan was off.

Maggie only got as far as the end of the hallway when she saw three boys, all friends of Alexia's, stalking toward the parking lot. "Bastard," she heard one of them say. It was Jeff, who had been vocal about his dislike of Kody for years. "A bastard and a demon," agreed another. Maggie felt her stomach clench. She had suspected that Kody's homecoming stunt with Alexia might cause problems, and he could be the only student they were talking about. Maggie turned to trail them, hanging back far enough that they wouldn't notice her. Her brain was screaming at her the whole time, "Not my business. Not my business. Not my business."

But somehow, Maggie felt that it was her business. She hating having anything like pity for Kody, but right now he was the only person she knew who was as ostracized as she was. He was also the only other person she knew who had to hide part of their physical appearance. Whether she liked it or not, she and Kody were united by their oddity.

Maggie saw Kody as soon as she reached the parking lot. He was leaning against the driver's side door of his car, his back to the school and Alexia's approaching friends. *He's waiting for me,* Maggie realized. *If he wasn't waiting for me, he would already be gone.* She felt a pang of guilt.

One of the boys ahead of her shouted, "Hey, demon!" and Kody turned slowly in response. They all picked up their pace, closing the distance to Kody's car quickly. Kody didn't move; he simply stared placidly at the boys, as if he was utterly unconcerned with them. Maggie could see the intent in the way each boy loped toward Kody, like a carnivore closing in on its prey, and she broke into a run to close the gap. By the time she was in earshot, the taunting had already begun.

Maggie reached the group right as Jeff, the biggest of the three, reached out and grabbed Kody's collar. Kody's expression remained calm, and Maggie could see that it only fueled Jeff's anger. Jeff said something to Kody so quietly that she couldn't hear it, but she saw Jeff's free hand curl into a fist.

Several things happened before Jeff could punch Kody. Maggie shouted "Stop it!" just as all three of Alexia's friends stumbled backwards, one of them actually falling to the ground. Kody jerked forward, his collar still tight in Jeff's grasp, but he wrenched himself free before he got pulled off balance.

Maggie, too angry to be afraid, marched around the car and stood in front of Jeff, her body blocking his path to Kody. Already, Jeff was preparing for another attack, his feet planted in a stance that suggested he was going to rush Kody. Maggie thrust her arm forward, her palm against Jeff's chest. "Stop it," she said again, her voice shaking.

Jeff's initial look of surprise quickly changed to one of pain, and he stepped back. "What are you doing to me? That burns!" He put his own hand where Maggie's had just been. "You're as much of a mutant as he is."

Without another word, Jeff turned and walked away. Reluctantly, his friends followed.

Maggie didn't wait for Kody to say anything. She simply crossed to the other side of the car and climbed into the passenger seat.

Like the first time Maggie had ridden with Kody to the old house, the drive was silent. But this time, instead of feeling like Kody was oblivious to her presence, Maggie felt like he was hyper aware of it. He glanced at Maggie so often that she suspected he was watching her even more than the road.

For her part, Maggie was no less uncomfortable. She knew Kody was going to be powerful, but seeing the bullies thrown backwards had been unsettling. They deserved it, she told herself, but it proved that the spell on Kody had locked down a lot more force than perhaps even he realized. If Kody's Talents were manifesting so quickly, what would he be like in a couple of days? In a month?

Maggie looked down at the hand she had laid on Jeff's chest, her thoughts finally turning from Kody's power to her own. When Kody had grabbed her arm the week before, he had flinched away the same way that Jeff had. Tentatively, Maggie put her hand against her cheek, but the skin was no warmer than usual. At least, Maggie told herself, it gave her something else to research in the hope of finding out what she was. She had gotten no closer to finding an answer, despite checking out a stack of books from the library the week before.

Kody remained still after he pulled his car to a stop outside his grandfather's house. He stared straight ahead as he said, "I didn't need any help, you know."

"Obviously." Maggie felt a surge of annoyance. Was she supposed to feel guilty for having rushed to intervene?

"I'm serious. I'm learning how to do more magic, and I could have handled them without you jumping in like that."

"Well, excuse me for coming to your defense. Clearly, I didn't think it through before I decided to put my face between yours and Jeff's fist."

Kody said nothing, and Maggie felt both the anger and the awkwardness between them growing. In an effort to ease the tension, she said, "What you did before I got there was impressive. I guess you've been finding new Talents already."

Kody finally turned to look at Maggie. "Are you kidding me?"

"No. You repelled three of them at once. I can't imagine that's easy."

"You don't have to imagine. You're the one who did it."

Maggie laughed sardonically. "Yeah, whatever. Other than having wings, I'm pretty much still a No Talent, remember?"

Kody shook his head. "You're not. You burned my hand the other day, and you did the same thing to that asshole jock back there."

Maggie shrugged. "A defense mechanism?"

"I think so. You're not even aware you're doing it, are you? And you didn't consciously think that you wanted Jeff and his buddies to go flying."

"Okay, maybe I do feel hot to the touch if I feel threatened. But don't forget, those guys were going after you, not me, so why would *I* have some sort of defensive reaction?" Maggie waited for Kody to answer. If she had repelled them unconsciously, then there was only one reason for it: she felt protective of Kody. There was no way Maggie was going to utter that idea out loud.

Apparently, neither was Kody. He abruptly opened his door and slid out of the car in one fluid motion. "Come on," he said. "Let's learn how to fly."

Maggie had dressed with flying in mind that morning. She had layered a tank top under a cardigan so she could manifest her wings without clothing getting in the way. Now, standing in the yard behind the house, she stripped off her cardigan and said, "Manifestum alae." There was still a stab of pain as the wings sprouted from her shoulder blades, but it was less than before. Maggie glanced over and saw that Kody was going through the same process, his shirt and leather jacket on the ground next to him.

"So, what now?" Maggie asked. "How do we actually get off the ground?"

Kody unfurled his wings, and Maggie had to step out of the way to avoid being hit by them. They looked even bigger in the daylight, and Kody closed his eyes in concentration before they began to move slowly back and forth. The motion sped up, and Maggie could feel the wind generated by each flap of his wings. Kody's wings beat faster and faster, but he remained firmly fixed to the ground.

"Maybe you need a running start," Maggie said, raising her voice over the sound of Kody's wings. "You know, like flying a kite."

Kody didn't even open his eyes. He simply began to run, straight toward the pond. Just before he reached the water's edge, his left foot thrust forward for his next stride and never touched the ground. Kody's legs were still making running motions as he rose into the air. Soon he was rising higher, and by the time he opened his eyes, he was thirty feet off the ground. Maggie could hear his whoop of delight as she stared, mesmerized.

Kody continued to fly in a straight line, then tentatively dipped his right wing while raising his left. He veered hard to the right and faltered, falling toward the surface of the pond before he righted himself. He tried turning again, moving his wings with more restraint, and soared toward Maggie. "How do I land?" he shouted as he passed above her head.

Kody circled back again, and the beat of his wings slowed. He got lower and lower, until his feet were just inches from the ground. He began to move his legs again, and his feet touched the earth as his wings ceased moving. It looked graceful at first, but Kody's forward momentum was too fast, and he pitched forward. Just before he landed face-first, he twisted his body and barrel-rolled along the ground, his wings folded in tight against his back.

Kody finally came to a stop on his back, and Maggie rushed over to him. "Are you okay?" she shouted.

Kody just laughed in answer, his face and chest streaked with dirt. "You should have repelled me so I didn't hit the ground so hard," he admonished, but he gave Maggie a wink. "You have to try this. It's the most amazing feeling ever."

Maggie nodded and stood, but after seeing Kody's painful first attempt, she was even more reluctant to leave the ground. Kody brushed himself off and stood up next to her. "When you want to turn, don't make any sudden movements. Just a little shift in your wings is all you need. And when you want to land, try to hover in one spot first. I think that will make it easier."

"Okay," Maggie agreed, but still her wings sat motionless.

"You can do this."

"Right." Maggie took a deep breath and mimicked Kody's earlier process. She unfurled her wings and began moving them back and forth, all of her concentration focused on their movement. When she felt that she couldn't flap them any faster, she began to run. Maggie took just three strides before she felt a cool breeze against her face, and suddenly her feet were dangling above the ground. Her wings felt buoyant, like they had caught the same breeze and were riding it upward. Maggie stopped beating her wings so hard, and she skimmed just a few feet above the ground. Soon she had reached the pond, and she risked a quick look down at the surface of the water. She saw her reflection, her body stiff with anxiety but her wings floating in a red haze on the water's surface.

Maggie shouted with excitement and moved faster, her wings taking her higher. When she cleared the tree line, she felt another breeze. It was cold, but it lifted

Maggie's wings, and she paused to let the wind carry her. She continued to rise, and she could see farmers' fields and woodland for miles. And, when she turned her head to the right, Maggie could see the water tower that stood near school. It was, Maggie decided, the happiest moment of her life. Let them tease me as much as they want at school, Maggie thought. They'll never be able to do what I can do.

Elated, Maggie continued to fly until she realized she would have to find her way back. She did as Kody had instructed, tilting one wing down just a few inches while raising the other. She turned gracefully, spied the pond up ahead, and made a beeline for it.

Kody met her halfway, flying at an even higher altitude. He fell into line next to Maggie, staying a safe distance away so their wings wouldn't be in danger of touching. Maggie turned and saw that Kody was grinning. Not the malicious smile she was used to seeing on his face, but an expression of absolute joy. Maggie realized that her face mirrored his.

Maggie and Kody continued flying for the next two hours. By the time the sun began to get low on the horizon, both of them had become much more adept at turning. Maggie could make tighter, more precise turns than Kody, but his speed outmatched hers. While Maggie's lithe red wings made her graceful and agile, Kody's substantial leathery ones gave him power.

Kody had perfected landing, too, though Maggie was still working to land without her knees buckling from the force. She tried to beat her wings rapidly just before touching down so the landing would be softer, but her timing was still a little off.

Eventually, Kody and Maggie settled in on the shore

of the pond, both out of breath from their efforts. Kody glanced up. "It's getting dark. I should probably take you home."

Maggie shook her head. "Just one more flight, okay?"

Kody just nodded his assent, and Maggie was in the air within seconds. The temperature was dropping, and she could feel goosebumps break out on her bare skin. Maggie spiraled up over the pond, her altitude growing with each loop. She glanced over and saw a few stars in the Eastern sky, sighed, and began to spiral down again.

Maggie was still far above the pond when she felt a sharp pain in her shoulder. She gasped as her wings faltered. Maggie refocused and moved her wings again, but the pain flared, even worse this time. Her shoulder was cramping from the long afternoon of flying. After hours of everything working so perfectly, Maggie suddenly couldn't get her wings to move in time with each other. Not knowing what else to do, she let them hang lifelessly behind her. Maggie looked down at the pond below her, prayed the water was deep enough, and fell.

CHAPTER 11

Maggie hit the surface of the water hard, the sting of the impact made worse by the sudden shock of the cold water. When she felt like her descent was over, she kicked hard toward the surface, but the weight of her clothes and her wings was overwhelming. Kicking even harder, Maggie managed to get her face above the surface. She sucked in a breath and said "oblitus alae" just before she slipped under again.

With her wings gone, Maggie was able to breach the surface again, and she looked wildly around her, wondering which direction would take her back to the house. She turned her gaze upwards at the sound of a shout and saw Kody deftly hovering above her. He reached down and grasped one of Maggie's hands, then began to fly toward the shore. Maggie kicked in time with Kody's wings, and as they got closer to the edge of the pond, she felt the ground underneath her feet. She slipped out of Kody's grasp and stumbled up onto the shore, her shoulder still aching and her entire body shivering with cold.

"Thanks," Maggie said quietly. She felt Kody's hand

on her arm, pulling her up.

"Come on, there are towels inside."

Maggie rose and followed Kody inside the cabin. When Kody flicked on the light, she could see that the place was neat and clean with surprisingly modern furnishings. Kody walked to a closet and pulled out two towels. "There's a dryer in the basement. You can put your clothes in there."

Maggie could feel her cheeks flush. "And I'm supposed to just be naked while they're drying?"

"Use a towel. Or I can take you home soaking wet. Your choice."

Staying wet and freezing wasn't an option Maggie wanted to consider, so she ducked into the bathroom, stripped off her clothes, and emerged with one towel wound tightly around her body and the second draped over her shoulders. "Not a word," she warned when she came out.

Kody opened his mouth to comment anyway, but a sudden flash of light made him turn toward the door. "Headlights," he said. "Someone's here."

"Your mom, maybe?"

"Not likely. The basement stairs are off the kitchen. Go put your clothes in the dryer and stay down there." Kody turned and walked out the door.

Maggie complied, shutting the basement door behind her. Once her clothes were spinning in the dryer, she crept back up the stairs and pressed her ear to the door. She didn't hear anything for a few minutes, then she distinctly heard the sound of a car starting and driving down the gravel road, away from the house. Maggie was surprised when, soon after the sounds of the first car had faded, she heard a second engine turn over and the crunch of wheels on the road. He's leaving me, Maggie thought. She felt a stab of panic, as if Kody had trapped her there at the house.

I'm not his prisoner, Maggie chided herself. I put myself in the basement, and if he's left, I can walk or fly home. Or call Bree.

With a shrug, Maggie settled onto a musty couch in one corner of the basement. She pulled her feet up under her body and curled up with her head on the armrest. The churning of the dryer was all she could hear, and she didn't fight the urge to close her eyes and sleep.

By the time Maggie awoke, the dryer had stopped and the basement was silent, but she was sure some noise had brought her to wakefulness. Shivering, Maggie jumped up and pulled her clothes out of the dryer. "Still warm," she pronounced, dressing in a hurry. She had just pulled on her tank top when she heard the basement door open. Kody stood there, his face as expressionless as usual.

"What happened?" Maggie asked.

"Some guy saw us. He came over to find out what was going on."

Maggie felt a sinking feeling. How could they have been so stupid as to think no one would see them up there in the sky? They should have stayed lower to the ground and closer to the cabin. "And?" Maggie prompted.

"And what? I told him that yeah, I can fly. He asked who I was with, and I said it was a friend who had flown home already. He noticed your sweater on the ground, but I told him you must have forgotten it. Here." Maggie hadn't noticed her cardigan in Kody's hand, but now he raised his arm and tossed it down the stairs to her. She slid into it gratefully.

"Thanks for covering for me," she said.

Kody nodded curtly and turned away. "Come on."

They were walking out of the house before Maggie asked, "Why did you leave?"

Kody shrugged. "Guy told me I should run on home

because it was a school night. He refused to leave until I'd gone."

"Nosy neighbor." Maggie shivered and hugged herself. "I don't think I'm ever going to get rid of this chill. That pond is freezing."

Wordlessly, Kody slid out of his leather jacket and handed it to Maggie. She eyed Kody as she put it on, still surprised at his rare moments of kindness. She should simply feel gratitude, she knew, but she couldn't help feeling a tinge of distrust, as if Kody was intentionally misleading her. You can't trust a half-demon, she thought. Then again, I don't even know what I am, so maybe I can't trust myself. That idea made Maggie shiver again, and she climbed into Kody's car feeling a mixture of exhaustion and fear.

Maggie had told her parents that she would be going to Shana's house that evening and just walking home, even though it was a three-mile trek. She hated lying to her parents but knew the truth wouldn't be at all acceptable. Kody dropped her off at Blue Fern Park, and Maggie walked home, feeling the soreness already settling into her muscles.

As she approached her front door, Maggie suddenly ran a hand through her hair, aware that it was still a tangled mess. She pulled a pencil out of her bookbag and hastily twisted it into her hair, forming a sloppy bun. If it was going to be wild looking, then she figured it should appear that she had intended to pull off that look.

Maggie had just closed the front door behind her when she realized that she had overlooked another important detail about her appearance.

"Where did you get that jacket?" Maggie heard her mother say, her tone suspicious.

Maggie was already formulating a lie, thinking she could claim it was Shana's, when her father strode into the room. "Finally! Sit down, right now."

Oh no, they know, Maggie thought wildly. Somebody else saw us, or Kody lied about covering for me. She dropped her bag and sat on the couch, inhaling deeply and fighting the urge to stand up and run.

"Your great-aunt Sarah insisted on communicating with me today," Maggie's mom began. "I have been trying to stay out of your business, but Sarah was practically hitting me over the head because she was so anxious about you."

Wendy stared at Maggie, as if waiting for a response. When Maggie just blinked and stared at the carpet, trying not to show her panic, her mom continued, "Do you know what she told me? That you've been hanging out with that demon boy. She said that you intervened in a fight he got into."

Maggie's head whipped up at those words. "Yes, I did. Three guys ganged up on him, and who knows what they would have done if I hadn't said anything."

"According to Sarah, the boy used his demon magic to handle it all just fine."

"At least I tried to help."

"He would have deserved whatever he got from those boys." Maggie turned to look at her father. She had never heard such malice in his voice. "Sarah also told your mother that you got in his car and left school with him."

"Is that true, Maggie?" Wendy asked.

"Yes." There was no point in denying it.

"Why? You've always hated him."

Maggie didn't answer; she didn't know what to say.

It was Richard who spoke next. "And didn't we tell you to steer clear of him?"

Maggie nodded.

"Then why were you with him today?"

Maggie suddenly felt indignant, and she sat up straight, her shoulders squared. "Because he doesn't judge me. Not anymore. I spent all afternoon with him, and not once did he call me a No Talent, and he never said that I wasn't good enough, or that I was just a late bloomer, or that I'm stupid because I have to take a freshman Readers class."

Both of Maggie's parents looked stricken. Clearly, whatever answer they had expected, that hadn't been it. Finally, Wendy said quietly, "You think we judge you?"

Maggie took a deep breath and let it out before she answered. "I think everyone at school judges me. I'm tired of getting teased all the time."

"But Kody teases you," Richard said.

"He used to, but I think he's finally coming around."

"You have Bree and Shana. They don't judge you."

"I know, but they're both really good at their Talents. With Kody…it just feels nice to be with someone like me."

Wendy's sympathy was quickly replaced with wariness. "What do you mean 'like me'? He's a demon."

"I mean," Maggie said, thinking quickly, "that he doesn't fit in. He's not like everyone else, and neither am I."

"That doesn't mean you're anything like him, though," Richard said. "If we ever hear that you've so much as spoken to that boy again, you will be grounded until Christmas vacation, do you understand?"

Maggie nodded, her heart sinking. As relieved as she was that great-aunt Sarah hadn't communicated anything about her wings, Maggie was hurt to hear Kody denounced so completely. *If they knew what I was,* she thought, *they would probably disown me. Or maybe they do know, and they're afraid I'll find out. If Sarah had been checking in on her, then why hadn't she* communicated the news of Maggie's wings? Of all the things she had done throughout the day, surely flying was the most shocking.

The next day, Maggie didn't see Kody again until lunch. He sidled up to her as she was walking toward the patio, skipping a greeting and simply opening with, "So, you want to go out again today?"

Maggie bit her lip, unsure what to say. She kept her eyes straight forward so she wouldn't have to meet Kody's gaze. "Um," she began, and stopped.

"What?"

"I got in trouble."

"For being out with me."

Maggie nodded, her eyes fixed on the herb garden in the distance. "My great-aunt Sarah told my parents I'd left school with you."

Even without looking at him, Maggie knew that Kody was frowning. "Your great-aunt Sarah was at school?"

"Her spirit apparently was. She died ten years ago, but she takes great delight in tattling on me to my mother. Mom's a Reader," she added.

"And if you go to the cabin with me again, she'll know, and you'll get in trouble because you're not allowed to hang out with me anymore."

"Yeah." Maggie finally brought her eyes up to Kody's. "I'm really sorry."

"You should tell your parents what you are. Maybe then they wouldn't be so worried about you being with me."

"But I don't know what I am. What am I supposed to say?"

"Show them your wings."

"No. No way." I'm not ready for that, Maggie thought, but another voice in her mind answered, "If not now, then when? They have to know someday." "No," Maggie said out loud, as much to reiterate her feelings to Kody as to still that inner voice.

Maggie had reached her usual table, and she put her backpack down. "Kody," she began hesitantly, "it's not just that I'm afraid of telling my parents. It's more than that." Maggie looked around her. Bree was already seated at the table, one eyebrow arched questioningly as she listened in. Students at surrounding tables were watching the exchange, too, probably because it was so rare to see Kody having a conversation with anyone, let alone with Maggie. "Follow me," Maggie said. Without waiting for Kody, she walked into the herb garden, not turning around until they were screened from view.

Kody was just a step behind, his mingled anger, disappointment and curiosity showing in turns on his face. "You can't tell anyone what I'm about to say," Maggie said.

Kody spread his hands. "Who am I going to tell?"

Despite her worry that telling Kody everything might not be a wise choice, Maggie plunged into the story about her visit to Healer Waltham's house. Kody's eyes grew larger with every repeated word of the Healer's, and when Maggie finished, he simply said, "What could make her react like that?"

Maggie shook her head. "Nothing I've ever heard of, and nothing I can find in any of the books I've checked out. Imagine if I just waltz into the living room one day with my wings showing. What if my parents freak out like the Healer did? They might not even want to let me live under their roof anymore. What if they're afraid of me?"

"I think I might be a little afraid of you." Kody's smile, though, said otherwise, and Maggie wasn't surprised that he was somehow pleased with the news. Kody's expression sobered as he added, "You were going to help me learn my Talents."

"I'm sorry," Maggie said again. "Maybe it's for the best that I can't help. If I did, Sarah might start communicating anything you do, too. I don't understand why she didn't tell my mom about my wings or the flying."

"You can thank my great-grandfather for that," Kody said. "He put a protective spell all around the property; no spirits can get across the barriers he set up. He grew up in a haunted house and hated all of the paranormal activity—he said it was annoying—so when he built the cabin, he made sure that no one would ever be able to haunt it."

"So if I go to the cabin, Sarah can't see what I'm doing," Maggie mused.

"But that doesn't solve how we're going to fly together if you can't go there in the first place."

Maggie sighed. "We just can't. That's all there is to it."

Kody shook his head. "That's not good enough." He paused, studying Maggie. "You don't like taking risks, do you?"

"I guess not. I don't know. I've never really had to take risks before."

"You're such a good girl," Kody said, pronouncing the last two words as if they put a bad taste in his mouth. "Or not, considering your current state."

Maggie could tell that Kody was slipping into his usual teasing. Before he could continue, she said, "Yeah, well, tell me when you figure out a master plan for us to keep practicing our flying. I've got to go. If Sarah sees me here with you, I'll be grounded."

"Tell your parents that I'm not the bad influence in this relationship," Kody said. Under the mocking tone,

Maggie could sense something else. Anger? No. Disappointment. Maggie was on the verge of apologizing again when Kody simply turned and walked away without another word.

CHAPTER 12

After school, Maggie retreated to her bedroom, her door firmly shut before either of her parents got home. Her mom knocked on the door at one point and offered a quiet, "How was your day, honey?" Otherwise, Maggie was left alone. She wasn't sure if her parents' obvious avoidance was a relief or a burden.

When she finally emerged for dinner, Maggie could feel the palpable tension in the dining room. Her mother was trying to act like her usual cheerful self, but it was awkward and exaggerated.

Maggie was not in the mood to help the situation. "So, did great-aunt Sarah check in on me again today?" she asked, piling mashed potatoes onto her plate.

"Not that I'm aware of," Wendy said tightly.

"What would she have seen if she had checked in on you?" Maggie's dad put down his fork and fixed his gaze on her.

"Richard!" Wendy admonished.

"It's a valid question. Maggie?"

"I told Kody we couldn't hang out anymore." Maggie had intended to make it a simple, matter-of-fact statement, but even she could hear the resentment in the words.

"Good," Richard said. He picked up his fork and resumed eating as if the matter was settled. "Are you still enjoying Readers class?"

Maggie gave a small shrug. "It's okay." She spent the next ten minutes shoveling food into her mouth as quickly as possible, anxious to be back in her room. Just as she took her last bite, one of the light bulbs in the fixture over the table began to dim. Maggie saw it and forced herself to take a deep breath. Nope, this can't happen right now, she told herself firmly. Calm down.

After several more deep breaths, the bulb returned to its usual appearance. "Can I go back to my room?" Maggie asked. "I need to finish my homework."

Wendy looked like she wanted to say something more, but she simply nodded her head. "Put your dishes in the sink first," Richard said absently.

Once she was back in her room, Maggie sprawled on her bed, staring up at the ceiling. If her overwrought emotions could make lights flicker and, according to Kody, repel people she felt threatened by, then maybe it was something she could learn to control. Maybe she could Manipulate consciously, whatever her emotional state was. Tentatively, Maggie raised a hand upward, focusing her gaze and her concentration on the overhead light. She narrowed her eyes, willing the bulb to dim, but nothing happened. Undaunted, she tried again and again, until she eventually fell asleep, still fully clothed. That night, she dreamed that she and Kody were flying over their school when a rainstorm blew in. Thick raindrops began to pelt her body and her wings faltered, but they kept beating. When the rain turned to hail, Maggie threw her arms over her head and began to fall.

Maggie sat straight up out of the dream, fully awake, but she could still hear the *plink* of hailstones bouncing against her window. Her bedroom was dark, and she assumed her mom had found her asleep and turned off the light. The brightest illumination in the room came from Maggie's alarm clock, which read 4:23 a.m.

Abruptly, the sound of the hailstorm outside ceased, and Maggie could hear a few late-season crickets chirping. Yawning, she slid out of bed and went to the window, pulling aside the curtain. The moon, just past its full, shone down from a clear sky, illuminating a dry lawn. Maggie frowned, wondering how the hail had melted so quickly and how the storm had dissipated in the time it took to cross her bedroom.

As she looked around, Maggie noticed something dark perched on her windowsill. She slid open her window and peered through the screen, but it was too dark to see what it was. Maggie turned on her bedroom light and went back to the window for another look. The object was a small black pouch, filled with something that smelled vaguely of cinnamon. Maggie recognized it as a spell bag of some sort, but why anyone would leave it on her windowsill was beyond her comprehension.

Too tired to think about it much at such an early hour, Maggie went back to bed, pausing only to change into her pajamas. It wasn't until she was settled under her covers that a new idea occurred to her. The hailstorm had only been in her dream, and the noise she had heard after waking had been someone standing outside her window, tapping on the glass.

Maggie was still awake when her alarm went off two hours later.

Maggie was bleary-eyed as she munched on a Pop-Tart the next morning. Her dad had already gone to work, and Wendy didn't seem to take much notice of

Maggie's steady stream of yawns.

Instead of heading straight to the bus stop at the end of the street, Maggie turned left as soon as she walked out of the house and circled around to her bedroom window. The black pouch was still there, and she scooped it up, quickly stashing it in her backpack. She edged her way to the front of the house again, hoping her mom hadn't noticed her quick detour.

Once she was on the bus, Maggie pulled the pouch out of her bag and examined it closely. It was made of a soft velvet fabric, and the top had been tied with twine. Maggie gave the pouch a gentle squeeze, and she could feel several small solid objects nestled in something grainy. From the smell, she guessed that ground-up cinnamon must be the grainy part. Cinnamon was used for protection spells and charms, she knew, but what made no sense was why someone would leave it on her windowsill in the middle of the night. Maggie vaguely wondered if her parents had put it there to protect her from Kody, but that didn't seem likely; they were worried about her going to see him, not vice versa. She wondered who might have left it, and why, all morning. When she brought the matter up to Bree and Shana at lunch, neither girl could offer a suggestion. It wasn't until the bell had rung to signal the end of lunch that Shana suddenly said, "Maybe it's not for your protection, Mags. Maybe someone is trying to protect themselves from you. Remember how scared that Healer was of you."

Maggie frowned, trying to picture Healer Waltham sneaking through the yard in the middle of the night. "No, that doesn't make sense. She could just carry it on herself if she wanted to ward me off."

"Cinnamon is also used for love spells," Bree interjected just as the girls prepared to split up for their respective classes. She drew out the word "love" in a singsong voice. "Maybe somebody has a crush on you."

"I'm not falling in love with anyone who's stalking around outside my window at four a.m.," Maggie said, though she giggled at the thought of anyone being that smitten with her. "See you guys after school."

Since the three girls had made plans to go to Bree's house that afternoon, they met up at the entrance to the student parking lot. Maggie got there first, and as she scanned the rows of cars, she realized that she was looking for Kody's car. There was no sign of it, and Maggie assumed he had left early. Probably heading out to his grandfather's cabin, Maggie told herself, and I should have been with him.

"You look dejected." Shana's voice broke through Maggie's musings, and she shrugged. "I just feel bad about Kody," she said.

Shana gave an incredulous laugh. "You have gone from hating him to feeling sorry for him, and everything in between, in the past two weeks. I can't keep up anymore."

"Me, neither. I guess it was just nice feeling like I could hang out with someone as weird as me."

"You're only weird because he tricked you into seeing the Healer. Besides, you're not weird, you're *special*. Like a snowflake. Our delicate, unique little snowflake."

Bree walked up at that moment. "Well, let's get our snowflake to my house before she melts. I want to see what's in that pouch."

Once they were in Bree's bedroom, the three girls perched in a circle on the bed, the pouch Maggie had found sitting in the middle of the circle. "So open it already," Bree urged.

"Are you sure I should?" Maggie asked. "They say that taking a talisman apart can undo its power."

"We don't know what kind of power this is," Shana

said. "I'm with Bree: it's better to find out what it is."

Maggie's answer was to pick up the pouch and unwind the twine. The black velvet was just a flat square of material that had been gathered, so she spread its edges out carefully. As she had assumed, roughly-grated cinnamon formed the bulk of its contents. Maggie reached out a finger and nudged a bay leaf poking out of the cinnamon.

Bree had grabbed a book titled "Herbs for Healing and Magic" out of the living room, and she flipped through it quickly. "Bay is also used for protection," she said, adding, "but not for love spells."

Between the three of them, they also identified a wilted piece of lettuce, several kernels of corn, and some small white objects that, judging by their smell, were slivers of onion.

By the time everything had been identified, Bree was nodding. "All things used for protection," she said. "Someone is definitely trying to keep you safe, Mags."

"But why? And from whom?"

No one had an answer for that, but Shana offered an optimistic, "At least we know it's not a creepy love spell."

The mystery of the pouch's contents and purpose, if not its maker, solved, Maggie carefully reassembled it before the girls turned reluctantly to their homework. Shana's assignment had been to practice levitating multiple objects in different parts of the room, so Bree and Maggie wound up watching more than working.

When she had finally succeeded in simultaneously lifting the nightstand lamp and a necklace on Bree's dresser, Shana raised her hands in surrender. "That's it. My last performance of the evening." Her proclamation was met with groans.

"What about you, Mags?" Bree asked. "Have you started moving beyond repelling slimy jerks like Jeff

Thackar?"

Maggie shrugged. "Nothing so far. Flying and fighting off jerks: those will be the Talents listed on my future job resume."

"I wish you had a Talent you could actually show off," Shana said thoughtfully. "It would make things easier for you at school."

Maggie agreed and admitted that she had been trying to explore other abilities with no luck. "Maybe one day I'll have had enough and just shout 'manifestum alae!' in the middle of Readers class." There was a pop and a crash as Maggie's wings manifested, ripping through the back of her t-shirt and knocking over the lamp that Shana had just been levitating. "Damn it! I didn't mean it! Oblitus alae!"

Bree and Shana were doubled over with laughter. "If you do that in class, you might take out some of the freshmen sitting near you," Bree said when her laughter had finally subsided into an occasional giggle.

"Yeah, and I don't want to ruin all of my shirts. I liked this one, too. Oh, well. You got one I can borrow, Bree?"

"Sure, hang on." Bree rummaged around in a drawer before pulling out a black t-shirt with a dramatic flourish. "This one was made for you!" The back of the shirt had an image of silver wings on it.

"Not as cool as my red ones, but a lot less destructive," Maggie said. "Thanks."

"Oh, speaking of destructive, have you guys seen what that angelic preacher is up to now?" When Bree and Maggie looked at Shana with surprise, she continued, "Look, my mom likes to watch his TV show sometimes, okay? But seriously, you two have to see this."

Shana pulled up a video on Bree's computer, and Maggie saw that even though it had only been posted three days before, the video had already been viewed more than four million times. "Talk about viral," Maggie said.

"Talk about nuts. Watch." Shana hit play, and Colin Buchanan suddenly began shouting at them from the screen. He was wearing another one of his perfectly tailored suits, but he was sweating profusely. He seemed to be in the middle of a zealous sermon. "I tell you, it is coming! The destruction of our age! My connection to the angels has given me this wisdom, and this wisdom is shouting 'War!' The calamity that will change our world is coming, and we must be prepared! We must be vigilant! We must be faithful that we will fight, and win, and face the new world that will await us on the other side! The angels are girding themselves with armor and sharpening their swords, even as we must! There is no escape! None! We must face this head on and..." Buchanan never finished his sentence. His face, which had grown more red as his fervor increased, suddenly grew still, and his eyes stared wildly across the top of his congregation. His body went slack, and he fell forward, unconscious, as the congregation erupted into screams of terror.

"Um, wow," Bree said.

"Yeah. Your mom likes this guy?" Maggie thought it seemed ridiculous.

Shana shrugged. "She says that Buchanan is entertaining. Anyway, Buchanan wouldn't be much good in a war if he can't even get through a speech without passing out."

"And it's already 6:30, so I'd better get home and start sharpening my sword," Maggie said, laughing.

Maggie made the same detour at home that she had in the morning, carefully replacing the black velvet bag on her windowsill. She didn't know if opening it had undone its magic, but now that she knew it was a protection spell, she figured it was best to leave it in place. Whoever had put it there, Maggie assumed they had her best interests at heart.

When she changed into her pajamas before bed, Maggie carefully folded the shirt that Bree had loaned her and put it in her backpack so she could return it. She glanced at Kody's leather jacket, which was draped across the back of her desk chair. She should take it back to him, she knew, but Kody was still avoiding her and showing up at school with his jacket would just prompt gossip. If he wanted it back, Maggie decided, he would just have to come and get it.

Kody might have been avoiding Maggie, but by third-period Readers class the next day, she realized that she was actively looking for him. She had stopped by her locker between each period, and she even took a route to Readers class that went by her old Naturals classroom. She chided herself when she realized that her excuses to stop by her locker had been just that: excuses to go in the hope that she might run into Kody.

Readers class banished all thoughts of Kody from Maggie's mind. They had progressed to the Celtic Cross spread of Tarot cards, used for answering specific questions. The class had divided into pairs, and a very reluctant boy had found himself stuck with Maggie as his partner. Ben dealt the cards and read them for Maggie, who was supposed to have a question in her mind. With every card he turned over, though, he made up a meaning to insult Maggie. "Oh, the Wheel of Fortune," he began, reading the first card. "That's a game show, but you would never win it because you're a senior who has to take freshman classes. The next one is the Ten of Wands. Ten, as in the grade you might actually get to next year while all the rest of your friends are starting college."

"Stop it," Maggie whispered with each derogatory comment. By the fifth card, she had had enough. "Shut up!" she hissed, leaning across the aisle. Ben rocked backwards, his head twisting violently like he had been struck across the face. When he straightened up, he looked at Maggie with mingled fear and surprise. Tentatively, he raised a hand to his nose. When he pulled his fingers away, there was blood on them.

Maggie gasped and felt panic rising in her chest. It had been one thing to repel Jeff when he had tried to attack Kody, but Ben had simply been insulting her, not threatening violence. The sight of Ben's bloody nose made it seem worse, too. I'm dangerous, Maggie thought wildly. Healer Waltham was right to be afraid.

"I thought you were a No Talent," Ben said, his voice thick.

"I am." Maggie opened her mouth to apologize, then checked herself. She wasn't ready to own up to what had just happened.

Ben eyed Maggie for a long moment, then got up and moved toward the front of the class. "Mrs. Simmons, Maggie gave me a nosebleed," he said loudly.

The entire class turned to look at Maggie, and she could feel her cheeks flush under their shocked stares. Maggie vaguely heard Mrs. Simmons say, "I highly doubt that, Ben. I think we all would have heard it if Maggie had punched you in the face. Get to the infirmary." A few of the students stifled laughs before they turned back to their work. "Maggie, just reshuffle the cards and read the spread for yourself."

Maggie nodded, relieved, but throughout the rest of the period she could feel Mrs. Simmons watching her closely. Did her teacher suspect her of having hurt Ben? Would she get in trouble for something she couldn't even control?

When the bell rang, Maggie quickly packed up and walked toward the door, but Mrs. Simmons called her name before she could escape. Once the rest of the students had left, Mrs. Simmons finally spoke. "Maggie, Talents usually manifest first as unconscious actions, things we can't control. Had Ben said something to anger you?"

A chain of events unfolded in Maggie's mind. If she said yes, then Mrs. Simmons would assume Maggie was finally showing aptitude in a Talent, and that would result in a phone call to her parents, and that would lead to more lying. "Maggie?" Mrs. Simmons prompted.

"I'd never even talked to Ben before today," Maggie said finally.

Mrs. Simmons nodded, but she peered at Maggie as if she knew the true answer. I'm so dumb, Maggie thought. I'm lying to a Readers teacher, who might be reading my mind right now. But even if she was, Mrs. Simmons simply gestured toward the door. "Get to lunch," she said, "and don't worry about Ben."

Maggie found it hard to comply with her teacher's suggestion that she not worry. Although Maggie was unconcerned for the boy and his nose, she was very concerned that this growing power would result in further accidents. A bloody nose was bad enough, but what might she be capable of if she was truly angry or in danger? Maggie's pensive mood made her quiet at lunch, and when Bree and Shana pried her for information, Maggie just answered vaguely that she had endured more teasing in Readers class. She felt guilty about withholding the full story from her best friends, but she had no idea how they would react if she told them how it had ended. The last thing she needed was to have her biggest supporters feel threatened by her uncontrollable ability.

The third time Bree saw Maggie turn to scan the patio, she sighed. "Mags, he's not out here."

"I haven't seen him since Monday."

"Which is what your parents want."

"But I need to talk to him." The words surprised Maggie, but she immediately knew they were true. She did need to talk to Kody. He had already seen some of her ability to repel someone, and she doubted that he would be afraid of what had happened in Readers. If there was anyone she could tell, it was Kody.

"Remember that rule we made a couple of weeks ago, when Maggie wasn't allowed to even think about that half-demon?" Shana said, her face turned to Bree while her eyes rested on Maggie.

"That was a good rule," agreed Bree. "But I have a better idea. You know how they say that if you have a song stuck in your head, you should listen to the song because that will get it unstuck? I think Mags needs to do that with Kody. He's like a song stuck inside her head, and she needs to go have a long chat with him and get it all out of her system."

"Hard to do when he's doing this disappearing act." Maggie frowned. "Has he even shown up at school at all since Monday?"

"Oh, yeah, I saw him in the parking lot this morning," Shana said. "And Bree is right. You need to get over this weird thing with Kody. Tomorrow night is the Halloween party at The Roundhouse. Everyone will be there, including him, I'm sure. We're going to find a nice quiet corner for the two of you to talk, and we'll make sure he can't escape."

Maggie sighed. Talking to Kody at a club was not what she had in mind, but it might be her only chance to actually see him, let alone tell him what was happening. "As long as we can find somewhere private."

"Agreed."

Chapter 13

Friday was Maggie's most uncomfortable day in Readers class since she had transferred there. Ben had pointedly moved to another desk, coercing another student into trading places with him. While Ben whispered to his classmates and gestured toward Maggie, the small boy who had moved into Ben's old spot slumped in his seat, as if he could make himself small enough to disappear entirely. He continually glanced at Maggie, never raising his eyes high enough to meet hers.

As Mrs. Simmons lectured at the front of the room, Maggie heard a soft noise in front of her. She looked down to see a folded scrap of notebook paper on her desk. She opened it tentatively, dreading what she might find inside. There was only one word written there: Freak. Maggie drew in a deep breath, her mortification growing as she heard the muffled snickers of Ben and his friends. When she exhaled, the lamps around the room suddenly flared brighter before returning to their usual dim glow. Maggie kept her face forward, fixed on Mrs. Simmons, willing herself to calm down. Everyone has to learn to control their Talent, Maggie told herself. I'm no different than anyone else.

The rest of the day was agonizingly slow, and Maggie found herself looking at the clock in each classroom more than her work. When the final bell rang, she bolted for the bus, ready to be away from anyone who might provoke her.

Maggie, Bree and Shana had agreed to be vampires for the Halloween party at The Roundhouse. Maggie had bought a pair of fangs for the occasion, and she wore her homecoming dress from her junior year, when she had gone to the dance with her two girlfriends. It was a short, black satin dress with spaghetti straps and a row of jewels across the top of the bust. Maggie added white powder to her face and an extra layer of black eyeliner. Halloween had never been Maggie's favorite holiday, and she was more anxious about finally talking to Kody than about what she was wearing.

At nearly eight o'clock, Maggie's mom knocked on the door. "Honey, Bree and Shana are here."

"Be right there." Maggie grabbed the small clutch purse that matched her dress and reached for the door handle, then paused. Without allowing herself to rethink the decision, she grabbed Kody's jacket, put it on and walked out.

Wendy and Richard were in the living room, and Richard raised an eyebrow. "Doesn't that belong to the demon?"

"I'm giving it back to him. Everybody will be at this party, including him, so Mom, don't let great-aunt Sarah flip out because of it."

Wendy nodded slightly. "We trust you not to disobey us." Her words sounded less like a vote of confidence and more like a warning. "Have fun, and be home by 11:30."

Bree and Shana were waiting outside, and Bree honked the horn as Maggie walked out the front door. "Lookin' good, blood-sucker!" Shana shouted out the passenger-side window.

Maggie slid into the backseat. "I feel like I have a lisp with these fangs."

"So just smile a lot and don't say anything at the party," Shana suggested, turning around to give Maggie a fanged grin. Maggie smiled back when she realized that Shana's words were distorted, too.

"Nice jacket," Bree said coolly, glancing at Maggie as she backed out of the driveway.

"You sound like my dad. Don't worry. I brought it with me so I can give it back to him. Let's go get this over with."

"Such Halloween spirit, Mags."

It felt like the entire school had turned out for the party at The Roundhouse, a club in an old railroad roundhouse on the edge of town. Bree had to drive two blocks down the street to find a parking space, and Maggie's feet were already tiring of her heels by the time they got in the door. The music inside was blaring, and Maggie could feel the bass pulsing in her chest. Moving deftly through the crowd of costumed bodies, Shana led the way to the dance floor.

Maggie didn't feel like dancing, but it was easier to stay on the dance floor than to try to find a seat somewhere. As Bree and Shana danced, Maggie moved in slow circles, her eyes searching the crowd for Kody. At one point, Bree leaned in and said, "You're going to make yourself dizzy! Be patient."

Someone wearing a blank white mask moved close to Maggie, getting so close to her that their faces nearly touched. Maggie recoiled, unnerved. The lights trained on the dance floor flashed, and Maggie caught a glimpse of blue eyes. Not Kody, then. Maggie turned away, but the masked face reappeared over her shoulder. A voice from under the mask said, "Mutant!" Maggie just bit her lip and kept her face turned in the opposite direction, determined not to react.

An hour slid slowly by, and eventually Bree and Shana tired of dancing. The three girls squeezed onto an old, sagging loveseat near the back of the club just as the music faded and the costume contest began. Maggie, still absorbed in trying to find Kody, wasn't even looking at the stage when Shana suddenly elbowed her. "Look!" Shana hissed.

"Where?" Maggie was peering at the people near them.

"Up there! On stage! Are those real?"

Maggie looked up and saw Kody standing at the center of the stage, a smug look on his face. He was wearing only jeans and a pair of beat-up combat boots, with his wings fully extended. They were so wide that other contestants had to back up to keep from being hit by them.

The entire crowd had fallen absolutely silent. Maggie stared, amazed at Kody's audacity. As far as she knew, he had kept his wings a secret from everyone else. And even though they knew what he was, seeing such solid proof of his demon heritage seemed to have dazed the crowd. They were so still that Maggie began to wonder if Kody had used his stunning skill on them. Then she saw a few people turn to whisper and heard someone give a shout of approval. Everyone erupted into cheering.

"Technically, he's cheating," said Shana, even though she joined in the applause. "He's not really in a costume."

"You should have entered, Mags," Bree said.

"Everyone would be cheering for you, too."

"No, thanks," Maggie mumbled. She was still staring at Kody, seemingly the only person there who wasn't clapping or shouting for him. She couldn't decide if what he had done was courageous or foolish, and she felt a stab of envy that Kody didn't have to hide his true nature. Maggie wondered how it must feel to stand up in front of everyone from school, hearing them roar their approval after years of insults and teasing. Kody's wings began to retract until they were folded against his back. He moved to the side of the stage to make way for the next contestant, but there was no doubt that he would be the winner. After five more contestants showed off their costumes, all looking crestfallen, the DJ announced Kody as the winner and handed him a giant trophy shaped like a bat. The trophy even looks like him, Maggie thought.

A song started playing as everyone returned to dancing, and Maggie turned to Bree and Shana. Before she could speak, Bree said, "We'll wait right here. Go get him out of your system."

Maggie walked toward the stairs at the side of the stage, but she realized she wasn't the only one heading that way. At least a dozen girls were already walking toward Kody, waiting to meet him as soon as he came off the stage. The bully who had always been an outsider was suddenly the most popular guy in school. A new emotion surged through Maggie, a tightening of her chest and a feeling like her heart had doubled its pace. Anger? Jealousy? Maggie stopped before she reached the group of girls, watching as they surged toward Kody, hands reaching out to stroke his wings. Kody observed all of them with narrowed eyes, a slight look of disgust on his face. He seemed to recognize the hypocrisy, too.

Kody looked up and saw Maggie standing there, wearing his jacket. He hesitated, then returned his attention to the girls around him. He slowly smiled and said something that Maggie couldn't hear. Moving together, the girls came even closer, and each one placed a hand against one of his wings. Then, as one, they all turned and walked away, silently. Kody watched them go before stalking out of a side door.

Maggie followed, knowing this was her chance to talk to Kody alone. She pushed past the girls who had just been thronging around him and slipped out the door. The alley outside was only dimly lit, but Maggie could see Kody a short distance away, leaning against a tall shipping crate. His trophy was sitting on the ground at his feet. As her vision adjusted, Maggie could see Kody's smirk. "I win a contest, and suddenly you want to talk to me again?"

"I've been wanting to talk to you all week."

"That's funny, because on Monday I'm pretty sure you told me to stay away from you."

"Look, I'm sorry about that, okay? It wasn't my decision."

"Yeah, you'd mentioned that. Can't think for yourself, I guess. Just like all those idiot girls."

"You used that trick on them. You made them touch you so you could put a thought in their heads."

Kody just smiled maliciously in response.

"Anyway, I can think for myself. I'm not supposed to talk to you, but here I am." Maggie felt her frustration growing. Kody had acted disappointed during their talk on Monday, but now that she was seeking his company, he seemed irritated by it.

"So talk."

It wasn't supposed to go like this, Maggie thought. I need that Kody I saw at the cabin, the one who I could actually have a conversation with. I need someone who will help me figure all of this out.

When Maggie remained silent, Kody prompted her

with, "Are you already not speaking to me again?"

"Can't you just be normal for once?" she countered.

Kody moved so quickly that Maggie didn't have time to take a step back. His body was suddenly against hers, his hands curled around her arms. Maggie could feel heat radiating off his bare chest as he sneered at her. "No, I can't be. In case you haven't noticed, I'm not normal. Ever."

"Neither am I!" Maggie's outburst broke the tension, and she saw Kody's eyes, so close to her own, soften. He let go of her and stepped back, running a hand through his hair self-consciously. Maggie continued in a softer voice, "That's why I need to talk to you."

Kody instantly looked alert. "Something happened to you. Some new Talent."

"Not new, just…worse." Maggie took a deep breath before she launched into her story about giving Ben a nosebleed. "I didn't mean to," she concluded. "I didn't mean to hurt him, and I couldn't tell anyone else because they would think I was a freak. They already do think I'm a freak."

Maggie closed her eyes as she felt a wave of shame wash over her. Shame for hurting Ben and shame as she realized that just a few weeks before, she had spat that same word at Kody. She felt a tear slide down her cheek, and she squeezed her eyes tighter, trying to hold back any more tears. "I'm sorry," she whispered.

"For crying in front of me again?"

"For being so mean to you."

"I was mean to you, too. I think we're even."

"What if I can't learn to control this?"

Maggie opened her eyes to find Kody standing close to her once again. "You're scared, aren't you?" he said softly.

"Yes."

Hesitantly, Kody put his hands on Maggie's arms

again, pulling her to him. He slid his arms around her shoulders, and Maggie rested her cheek against his collarbone. She returned the embrace, her arms tight around Kody's waist. It felt strange but comforting at the same time. Despite her enmity with Kody, he was the one person who knew how dangerous she might be, and yet he accepted it—accepted her—without question. Maggie felt her shoulders begin to relax, the tension of the past couple of weeks slowly draining out of her. Unburdening herself to someone so completely made Maggie feel physically lighter.

Maggie felt Kody's wings brush her forearms as he shifted. "We have to practice together," he said firmly. "I don't care how we do it, or how we hide it from your great-whoever, but we have to. It's better than you blowing up someone in the middle of class."

"Agreed."

Kody slowly began to let go of Maggie. "You'd better go back in before your bodyguards come looking for you."

"They're not that over-protective of me," Maggie said.

Kody raised one eyebrow skeptically. "I'm more afraid of them than I am of you. I'm heading out. I got my trophy, so there's no point in sticking around. I'll think of some way for us to practice without anyone finding out. See you Monday."

"Bye, Kody. Thanks." Maggie turned back toward the door as Kody scooped up his trophy and moved toward the end of the alley. She had just reached the door when she realized she was still wearing his jacket. Shaking her head, she turned back and was about to shout Kody's name when she saw three figures moving up the alley toward him.

Something about their stance put Maggie on alert, and she stepped behind a dumpster so she could watch without being seen. The leader of the three had on a white mask, which he lowered as he approached Kody. Jeff. So he had been the one taunting her on the dance floor. Maggie felt a surge of rage. It wasn't fair that a guy like that was allowed to get away with being such a jerk and a bully.

Jeff kept walking until he was a foot from Kody. His two friends closed in and stood slightly behind Kody, trapping him.

Maggie stepped out from behind the dumpster, ready to intervene just as she had done in the parking lot. Between the shadows and Jeff's intense focus on Kody, no one realized she was standing there. Just as she began to walk toward them, Maggie checked herself. Kody had been angry with her for coming to his aid against Jeff before, so why would now be any different? "Boys and their stupid pride," she muttered to herself. She stayed where she was, watching as Jeff spoke in a low voice to Kody. She couldn't hear what he was saying, but his body language suggested that he was threatening Kody.

Even though she was expecting it, Maggie still gasped when Jeff suddenly raised his right fist and punched Kody hard in the face. Kody reeled backward, but he caught himself and faced Jeff again. Jeff's arm flew forward in another punch, but Kody smoothly dodged it as his own fist made contact with Jeff's stomach. Jeff doubled over, the wind knocked out of him, and Kody raised his arm again, aiming for Jeff's face. Before he could connect, though, the other two boys grabbed Kody, each pinning one of his arms behind him tightly, crushing Kody's wings against his back.

Jeff, wheezing, straightened up and punched Kody in the face again. Maggie put a hand to her mouth to keep from crying out as she watched Kody trying unsuccessfully to wrench himself away from the others. Unable to fight back or defend himself, Kody could only watch as Jeff punched him again, this time in the ribs.

Suddenly, the boys holding Kody let go, dropping his arms in unison. "Come on, Jeff, he's not worth it," said one.

"Shut up and hold him!" Jeff shouted, his hand already poised for another blow.

"We're going back inside." The two boys turned and began walking away. Maggie darted back behind the dumpster just in time to avoid being seen, listening as their footsteps passed on the other side.

Distracted by the desertion of his friends, Jeff didn't realize how close Kody had moved to him. Kody's hand darted out, not to punch but to lightly touch Jeff's shoulder. Jeff gave him a confused look, then his eyes unfocused. After a few tense seconds, Jeff's face slackened and his arms fell limp by his sides. He sidestepped Kody and followed the other two bullies toward the side door of the club, while Kody headed for the alley's entrance without looking back.

Maggie was impressed by Kody's quick thinking and his clever way of ending the fight, but she was still angry with Jeff. Between his hatred of Kody for simply being a half-demon and his disgust of her for being a No Talent, Maggie had lost any concern she might have felt for Jeff. He deserved to get his ass kicked, Maggie thought, and Kody let him go. It's not fair. Jeff can't keep getting away with this. He deserves to lose in a way that really hurts.

As she thought those words, Maggie heard an agonized shout and a crashing sound. Yells followed, and Maggie risked a peek around the side of the dumpster to see what had happened. Jeff was lying on the ground, writhing in pain. His two friends had run back to him, bending over him and asking again and again, "What? What happened?"

"My leg!" Jeff finally croaked out. Maggie looked

and saw that the lower part of Jeff's left leg was bent at a funny angle. It was clearly broken. Had he tripped and fallen? Maggie wanted to believe that, but she knew better.

Feeling her own panic begin to rise, Maggie backed down the side of the alley, sticking close to the club's outer wall to stay in the shadows. She moved quietly, watching as one of Jeff's friends ran inside, presumably to get help.

Maggie reached the end of the alley, her back still to the street beyond. Hoping no one would see her exit, she whirled around and found Kody right in front of her, his eyes wide. "What did you do?" he whispered.

Maggie just shook her head, too unnerved to respond.

"Come on." Kody grabbed Maggie's hand, glanced around, and hustled her across the street. Maggie was relieved when she saw that no one was standing in front of the club, and she expected Kody to stop moving once they were deep into an abandoned warehouse. His pace didn't slacken, though, and they emerged onto another street, one that was darker and had fewer cars parked along the curb. Kody turned left and continued moving until they reached another alley. He ducked into it and stopped halfway down, finally releasing Maggie's hand.

"I broke his leg," Maggie blurted.

"Did he see you?"

"No, I was hidden. I wasn't even looking at him when it happened. It was an accident."

"Your 'accidents' are getting worse, and I'm going to get blamed for this one." Instead of sounding angry, Kody's tone was straightforward.

"I'll tell Jeff it was me."

"No."

"I can't let him blame you for this. He hates you enough as it is."

Kody paused, biting his fingernails unconsciously as

he thought. "Actually, I doubt that he'll say anything about it," he finally said. "I don't know that Jeff would ever admit to getting hurt by me. It would kill his reputation."

"Even if he doesn't tell anyone, he's going to want revenge," Maggie said.

Kody gave a nonchalant wave. "Let him try. He can't hurt me."

"He did tonight. Are you okay?" Maggie peered at Kody's face, but it was too dark to see him clearly.

"I'm fine. Look, you don't need to go back in there tonight. Text one of your girls and tell them I'm taking you home."

"That will not go over well."

"You'd rather go back inside, where everybody will be talking about what just happened? They'll start asking where you've been all this time."

Maggie was about to point out that she was a No Talent, so no one would suspect her anyway, when she heard the distant sound of a siren. An ambulance on its way for Jeff, she was sure. Even in the dim light, Maggie could see Kody's eyes widen as he glanced anxiously toward the street. Kody's insistence on her not going back inside suddenly made sense. He wasn't worried about Maggie being accused of hurting Jeff; he was worried that she would implicate him if she started telling others about what had happened in the alley.

Maggie texted Bree, still too upset to argue. She knew she would have to answer a lot of questions from both Bree and Shana later.

Bree texted back almost immediately. She had typed "BE CAREFUL" followed by half a dozen exclamation points and then, "It just got crazy here. Fill you in later."

"Where are you parked?" Maggie asked, cramming her phone into her purse.

Kody snickered. "Parked? I flew. Break out your

wings."

"Are you kidding? No way. We might be seen."

Kody shook his head firmly. "No. We'll fly up high, it's dark, and it's late. You're not allowed to make any excuses this time. You need to get home, and you're getting there by flying."

"This is a bad idea," Maggie mumbled, even as she began slipping out of Kody's jacket. "Oh, this is yours. Here." Once it was in Kody's hands, Maggie wiggled and tugged at the back of her dress, ensuring that it was out of the way for her wings. "Manifestum alae," she said. Once her wings appeared, Maggie stretched them out, enjoying the feel of the cool night air against them.

Kody stepped back and smiled appreciatively. "Nice look, No Talent," he said. When Maggie just gave him a confused look, he continued. "The red wings, the dress, the fangs. Lucky for me you didn't enter the costume contest."

Maggie knew she was blushing under her pale make-up, and she was glad that Kody couldn't see it in the darkness. An awkward silence stretched between them, broken by the sound of a giggle. They both turned to the mouth of the alley to see Alexia Maynard, hand-in-hand with one of the boys from the football team. "Oops," she said, giggling again, "it looks like this spot is taken."

Alexia's date suddenly started toward Kody, but Alexia pulled him back. "Taylor, what are you doing?"

"It's the demon. I'm going to kick his ass. And look who his date is. What's wrong, demon, couldn't trick Alexia into going out with you again?" Taylor continued struggling against Alexia's grip until he wriggled his way free and sprinted down the alley. Taylor stopped as he neared them, his anger toward Kody forgotten as he stared at Maggie. *Not at me*, Maggie thought. *At my wings.*

Kody put his hand on Taylor's arm. Taylor mumbled,

"Nice costume," to Maggie and turned. Alexia caught up with him just then, and she gaped at Maggie, too. When Kody tried to touch her, she flinched and stepped back.

"You've got to do it," Kody said under his breath to Maggie.

"Come on, I'm heading back inside," Maggie said. She gently steered Alexia around, one hand on her arm. They had only taken a few steps when Alexia began staring at Maggie's wings again. Maggie was trying to emulate Kody's magic, trying to plant a different thought in Alexia's head, but it wasn't working.

Maggie heard Kody's voice in her ear. "See it, see the thought you want her to have. Then see that thought traveling through you and into her, all the way up to her little brain." Maggie concentrated harder, visualizing the thought transfer as Kody instructed. Slowly, Alexia's head turned away from Maggie and faced forward. "Nice costume, No Talent. Taylor, take me back inside."

Taylor complied, and Maggie gratefully watched them go. Despite the close call, she was smiling when she turned to Kody. She wanted to shout she was so happy about finding a new magical ability, though she wondered if she could replicate it if she wasn't under duress.

Kody smiled back at Maggie. "And this is why we need to practice together. We're both going to learn a lot more if we team up."

Maggie agreed, and she felt excited at the thought of learning more. For the first time, she wasn't worried about getting in trouble with her parents. She wanted to learn more magic, and she wanted to learn it with Kody.

"We should go before anyone else sees us," Kody said, pulling Maggie deeper into the alley again.

Maggie stripped off her heels, held them in one hand, and ran, hoping her feet would find the cleanest patches of asphalt. She had to flap her wings hard since there was no helping breeze in the alley, but as soon as she cleared the buildings on either side, a gust caught her wings and lifted her an extra fifty feet. Maggie could hear Kody just behind her, his wings making a soft rustle with every beat.

"Which way?" she shouted, trying to get her bearings as she looked at the buildings and streets below.

Kody overtook Maggie easily, then veered right. They continued to climb until the cars driving around the outskirts of town looked like little wind-up toys. Maggie loved the feeling of being in the air, and she hoped this flight wouldn't end like the last one. Crashing into a pond had been bad enough, but as they flew closer to downtown, there wasn't even a field to land in.

Maggie began to recognize landmarks, and she instinctively started to decrease her altitude in sync with Kody as they neared her neighborhood. They spiraled down over Blue Fern Park, knowing it would be the most secluded place to land. Maggie stumbled a little when her bare feet hit the grass, but she gave one final flap of her wings to rebalance herself. Kody, on the other hand, landed with ease.

"You've been practicing," she said after her wings were hidden once again.

Kody nodded. "I've learned some new magic, too. Come on, I'll walk you home." He raised a warning finger. "And don't you dare argue. After the night you've had, there is no way I'm leaving you by yourself."

Maggie silently agreed, and as she put her heels back on, she suddenly realized that her bed was the place she most wanted to be. She and Kody said little on the walk to her house. A few trick-or-treaters rushed past them as they turned onto Maggie's street, and Maggie jumped when one of them shouted incoherently. "And this is why I didn't let you walk by yourself," Kody said.

"Relax. Stop freaking out and just be glad it wasn't worse."

Maggie stopped. "I wanted it to be worse," she said quietly. "In my head, I wanted him to be bleeding and unconscious on the ground. Isn't that awful?"

"Coming from someone like you, it's pretty extreme," Kody agreed. Maggie could hear the surprise in his voice. "I want to practice magic with you, but remind me not to let you try anything on me."

"I've thought that kind of stuff before. I mean, we all do, right? People would tease me so much, and I'd just think, 'I wish they'd wake up tomorrow morning with their mouths missing.' But I never truly *wanted* that to happen. It's just…a fantasy."

"I know you didn't mean to actually hurt Jeff, and I know you feel guilty about it. You have to cut yourself some slack. You still have to learn to control your abilities."

"That's what I'm worried about. Maybe I am learning to control my abilities. First it was just pushing someone away, then it was a nose bleed, now it's breaking bones. I'll wind up killing someone next!" Maggie hadn't realized that she had grabbed Kody's wrist until she felt him gently prying her fingers away.

"No, you'll just learn to use your magic on purpose, consciously, like you did with Alexia."

"Why would I ever hurt someone on purpose?"

Kody had no answer for that, so he simply began walking again. He and Maggie remained silent until they reached the house next to hers. "You'd better leave me here," she said. "Thanks for bringing me home."

"Try not to maim anybody between now and Monday, okay?" Kody ran into the street and flew above the trees before Maggie could even think of a retort.

Maggie unlocked the front door and went inside as quietly as she could, hoping her parents might already be in bed. As soon as she heard a deep voice coming from the living room, she knew someone was still up, watching TV. Steeling herself against any questions about the evening, Maggie walked in and found her mom curled up on the couch, staring with wide eyes at the TV. Maggie followed her gaze and was surprised to see the now-familiar image of Colin Buchanan on the screen. He was shouting and sweating as much as ever.

"It is here! Take heed, my faithful flock, and pray that we will be spared in the carnage that is to come!" Buchanan was waving a fist in the air.

"I didn't know you were a fan of his," Maggie said.

Wendy jerked upright, glanced at Maggie, and rushed to turn off the TV. "Maggie, honey, I didn't hear you come in. How was the Halloween party?"

Maggie paused, searching for something that was at least somewhat truthful. "Spooky," she finally said.

"I see you got rid of that jacket."

"Yep. And on that note, I'm off to bed. Night, Mom."

"Good night, honey." Wendy sounded distracted, and as she walked down the hallway to her bedroom, Maggie heard the TV click on again. The last words she heard before shutting her door were, "The war between the angels and the demons has begun!"

CHAPTER 14

Maggie woke up early the next morning wondering how long Jeff had spent at the hospital and how badly broken his leg was. She tried to think of anything other than the previous night, but the sound of his cry when she had hurt him kept coming back to her. With a huff, she got out of bed, dressed, and grabbed her book, hoping that getting lost in a novel would help. The sun was shining through her window, so Maggie decided to head to the park.

Maggie opened the front door, and she glanced down to see that something bulky was sitting on the doormat. She screamed when she realized it was the body of a dead goat.

Wendy and Richard came running as Maggie stood there, horrified. She simply pointed at the animal in response to their inquiries. Wendy gagged and covered her mouth, but Richard was silent. Eventually he just said, "Wendy, go get a garbage bag. Maggie, go inside."

Maggie complied, her mind feeling numb. She sat down on the couch and was vaguely aware that her mother had sat down next to her, taking Maggie's hand in her own. It wasn't until Richard came in and announced, "It's in the trash," that Maggie finally looked up. "The poor thing had had its throat slit," he continued. "There was hardly any blood."

"Why was it on our front porch?" Maggie blinked hard in an effort to erase the scene that kept replaying in her mind.

"Some kid's idea of a Halloween joke, probably." Richard sounded less confident now.

"It wasn't there when I came home last night."

"Well, I'm just sorry you had to find it, Maggie. Now that we're up, why don't we have some breakfast?"

Maggie shook her head. "I don't think I could eat anything right now. I'm going to go to the park and read."

Maggie reached Blue Fern Park and just kept walking. She wasn't even sure where she was going, but her mind was too restless for her body to be still. The sickening angle of Jeff's broken leg, the image of the dead goat, and Kody's quiet voice asking, "You're scared, aren't you?" were playing on a constant loop in her head. Maggie wanted to scream, feeling like her brain was going to explode with all of the fear and confusion inside it. It was only when her stomach started to growl that Maggie stopped and realized just how far she had walked from home. She sighed, wishing she could fly in broad daylight and not give a damn, and turned to make the trek home.

Maggie finally walked in the front door well after lunchtime and stopped short when she went into the living room. The coffee table was piled with things, but the most notable was a vase with at least two-dozen red roses in it.

"Mom?" Maggie said, hearing Wendy enter the room behind her.

"For you," Wendy said.

"Who sent me flowers?" Maggie picked up the small card nestled among the stems, but it had only her name on it, written in a flowing script with gold ink. She flipped it over, but the back was blank, too.

"Not just the flowers. All of it. I opened the door and the flowers were there. Twenty minutes later, I went to put something in the mailbox, and there was more stuff. Every single thing has your name on it." Wendy looked searchingly at Maggie. "Who is he?"

"What?"

"Who's the boy sending you all these things?"

Maggie laughed uncomfortably. "Mom, there is no boy, trust me. This must be some kind of weird joke." She sat down and began pulling boxes toward her. One contained half a dozen cupcakes, while another was full of chocolates. A third package, wrapped in brown craft paper, turned out to be a hardback copy of Dracula. Inside, the flyleaf was inscribed with "Happy Halloween, Maggie!"

"I don't get it," Maggie said, pulling a pretty sun catcher out of a pink bag. "Why would someone do this to me? I mean, it's all very nice, but it has to be a joke."

Wendy just sighed and shook her head. Without a word, she turned and walked to the kitchen, reappearing a few minutes later with a sandwich and chips on a plate. "You haven't eaten," she said simply.

Despite her hunger, Maggie ate slowly, hardly paying attention to her food as she stared at the gifts before her. They were actually nice presents, not the kind of thing she would expect to get if it was a joke. But who would send her these things anonymously? And why?

After she ate, Maggie called Shana and Bree, asking both of them to come over. "You have to see this," she said, refusing to give any more detail.

The two girls were as mystified as Maggie and equally horrified about the dead goat. "Do you think the person who left the goat also left the presents?" Bree asked. "Maybe the goat was a joke, but then they felt bad about it and are trying to make it up to you."

Maggie shrugged. "It's as good a theory as any."

"Maybe Kody sent them," Shana said, her voice barely above a whisper.

Maggie threw a look at Shana to keep her from saying more, and Bree piped up in a loud voice, "Let's get you some fresh air. You need it." Before she could protest, Bree pulled Maggie up off the couch.

A tiny box was sitting on the front porch, occupying the same spot that the goat had earlier. Maggie hadn't even heard anyone approach the house, and she picked up the box warily. It was a covered in a deep red velvet, and inside was a pair of delicate diamond earrings. "This is nuts," was Maggie's only response. "Whoever's doing this is going way too far."

"Yeah, it's not funny," agreed Shana. "They need to back off."

Maggie shoved the box in her pocket and kept walking. As soon as they were away from the house, Bree began asking questions about Maggie's conversation with Kody.

"He was kind of a jerk at first," she conceded, "but then I think he started to understand that, you know, I feel bad about not being able to hang out with him."

"And then you let him take you home," Shana prompted.

"We flew home," Maggie said. "We landed in the park, and then he walked me to the house."

Shana cleared her throat in a way that showed her disapproval, but Bree nodded knowingly, her eyes teasing. "You can't blame him for falling for the sexy vampire." When Maggie didn't laugh, Bree peered at Maggie suspiciously. "There's more you're not telling us. So tell us."

Maggie glanced around to make sure no neighbors were in earshot. She took a deep breath while holding an internal debate. Bree and Shana were her best friends, and she was already hiding the incident with Ben from them. It was the first secret she could remember ever keeping from Bree and Shana. Should she tell them what had happened with Jeff? Would they be terrified of her? There was only one way to find out.

Haltingly, Maggie told them what had happened. She was shaking by the time she finished her story. "All this time I was worried about how dangerous Kody would be with his demonic abilities, and it turns out I'm the evil one," she concluded.

Bree and Shana both had shocked expressions on their faces, but their obvious concern for Maggie softened their features. As one, they leaned in and put their arms around Maggie. "I won't pretend that I'm not freaked out by this," said Shana, "but we know you would never do something like that on purpose."

"Besides, Jeff is a jerk and he deserved it," added Bree.

"Bree!" Maggie exclaimed. "You never say things like that."

"It's true, though."

"You guys don't hate me?" Despite their reassurances, Maggie was still afraid.

"Promise," Bree said.

"Are you going to start going out with Kody?" Shana asked suddenly to change the subject.

Maggie smiled for the first time that day, and she raised one eyebrow wryly. "Only if he keeps walking around shirtless like he did last night."

"Oh, I'm glad somebody said it. He looked hot." Shana pretended to swoon as Maggie swatted at her playfully.

Maggie made a beeline for her room when she was

alone again. She had been relieved that no more presents were waiting on the porch when she got home, and she buried the box with the earrings in it under a pile of socks in her dresser. It was an expensive gift, and as uncomfortable as it made her feel, she could only imagine how her parents might react to it. She thought about calling Kody to ask if he was behind it, then discarded the idea. For one thing, she didn't even have his phone number, and for another, she was certain that if Kody had any romantic interest in her, this wouldn't be the way he would show it.

The evening passed quietly, although conversation at dinner was stilted. Maggie almost laughed when she realized that she wished she could go back a month in time, when her biggest problem was having not yet developed a Talent.

That night, Maggie dreamed she was in a small boat floating in a sea of blood. Presents kept dropping out of the sky into the boat, making it list violently with every new delivery. As the presents piled up, Maggie had to climb on top of them to keep from getting buried underneath the bigger boxes. She tried throwing them overboard, but they would always slip out of her hands. Maggie woke up just as the weight became too much and the boat began to sink.

The sun was shining brightly through her window, and Maggie was surprised to see that it was already ten o'clock. She had slept for twelve hours.

Wendy and Richard had left a note that they had gone out to run errands, and Maggie was glad to have the house to herself for a while. She stretched out on the couch with a bowl of cereal and watched an old B-movie about a robot uprising. Much better than blood and presents, Maggie thought. That mental image reminded Maggie of the day before, and she went to the front door, steeling herself for what she might find there. The doorstep was bare. Maggie let out the breath she didn't know she had been holding.

An hour later, after getting showered and dressed, Maggie opened the door again, this time to walk to the library so she could finish an essay for World History. Maggie looked down and groaned: a silver tray piled with fruit had been placed on the ground. "You're killing me!" Maggie said to no one in particular. As she reached down to retrieve the tray, a small stone clattered near her feet. Maggie looked up just as another one grazed her arm. She looked in the direction that the stones had come from and saw a pale face obstructed by dark hair peeking from behind an oak tree.

"My parents aren't home," Maggie said.

Kody emerged from behind the tree, a sheepish expression on his face. "I wasn't sure," he said.

"That doesn't mean the neighbors aren't going to notice, though. Hang on." Maggie put the tray inside the house and locked up the door. "I'm heading to the library."

"And I'm heading wherever you are." Kody's tone was matter-of-fact. "What's with the fruit?"

"It's a long story. So you've thought of a way for us to practice together without being seen?"

"No."

Maggie questioned Kody unsuccessfully until they were three blocks away, when Kody turned left. "Change of plans. We're not going to the library."

There was something about Kody's manner that frightened Maggie, an urgency she had never seen in him before. Her essay forgotten, Maggie followed Kody to where he had parked his car. She slid in and knew without asking that they were going to his grandfather's cabin.

"I sure hope my great-aunt Sarah doesn't see this," Maggie said, trying to bring some levity to the tense energy inside the car.

"I kind of hope she does." Kody's answer was unexpected. "You need someone keeping an eye on you."

Maggie frowned. "Are you referring to the fact that I might accidentally maim someone if I don't have a chaperone?"

"I think you're in danger, and I don't mean from yourself."

Chapter 15

Kody lapsed into silence again, answering Maggie's inquiries with a solemn, "Wait." Maggie waited impatiently for what seemed like a longer-than-usual drive, her leg bouncing up and down and her fingers tapping against the armrest. Finally, Kody turned and drove through the sunflower field that led to the cabin.

Once they parked and got out of the car, Kody bypassed his favorite spot on the back porch and went inside, settling onto the couch. Maggie sat on the opposite end of it, her eyebrows raised in a silent prompt.

"Your bedroom is on the back right corner of the house," Kody stated.

"How do you know that?"

"Because something was standing outside your window last night."

"Some...thing?"

"Something with wings. It was too dark to see what they looked like. I could just make out the shape."

Despite the warmth of the cabin, Maggie shivered. "Was it trying to break into my room?"

"It was just standing there, not moving. It was facing outward, like it was guarding you."

"If it was guarding me, then why do you think I'm in danger?"

Kody gave Maggie an exasperated look. "I thought you were supposed to be one of the smartest people in our class. If you're being guarded, then that means someone is trying to hurt you."

"I woke up one night, a couple of weeks ago, and someone had been outside my window. They left a charm bag for protection." Maggie fell silent, thinking about the events of the past few weeks. "It showed up the night after we went flying together the first time."

"Someone knows what you are."

"At least two someones must know. The someone who wants to hurt me, and the someone who's guarding me. Who are they, and why do they even care?"

"I don't know. But you have to be careful. I know you like napping—"

"Daydreaming," Maggie interjected.

"—in parks, but you shouldn't be out alone."

Maggie suddenly felt very isolated, sitting in an old cabin so far from the rest of town. "What happens if they attack us here?"

"You've got me. And your own ability, too." Kody paused. "I brought you here because I didn't want anyone, living or dead, to overhear us. But we should stay and practice together. I think you're going to need all the practice you can get."

"Yeah, okay, for a little while."

The practice session turned out to be a frustrating one for Maggie. No matter what she tried to do, nothing would happen. Kody, on the other hand, was rapidly improving, and Maggie was reminded of Healer Waltham's admonition for her to keep an eye on him. He had only been free of his binding spell for a week, and already he was doing advanced magic. Maggie watched, impressed, as Kody levitated three plates in the kitchen.

"It took years for Shana to levitate anything that smoothly," Maggie conceded.

"I want to try some other Manipulator skills, too. Let's go outside."

Maggie followed Kody outside to the edge of the pond. Kody turned his eyes on a patch of grass sticking up at the edge of the water. His brow furrowed in concentration, but nothing seemed to be happening. Just as she was about to ask what he was actually trying to do, Kody let out a low laugh. The grass was wilting, turning black and bending limply as they watched.

"Great, you're the guy who can kill grass," Maggie said sardonically.

"If I can kill grass, what else can I kill?"

"Nope. None of that talk around me. Just because you're a half-demon doesn't mean you have to go around acting like one."

"What if that someone who's after you does attack us here? Don't you want to know I could keep you safe?"

"I want to know we could beat it and get away, not kill it."

Kody shook his head and gestured to her. "You try it."

Maggie stared at another clump of grass, willing it to die. "Nothing's happening," she finally said.

"Touch it. My powers began manifesting when I was touching the thing I was using magic on."

Maggie felt foolish putting her fingers against the grass, but she complied. Again, nothing happened. Kody came closer and knelt beside her. "See it in your head," he began. "See it dying, then send that image down your arm and into the grass." He traced a line with his finger, starting below Maggie's ear and down the length of her arm. Maggie focused again, and slowly, the grass began to wither. When half of it had turned brown, she finally gave up. "It's a start," she said meekly.

"You'll eventually learn to control your magic without feeling scared or angry. You felt hot that one time when you were mad at me. Try it again. Put your hand against me."

Maggie put her hand on Kody's shoulder, gathering all of the angry thoughts about Kody that she could. She reminded herself of all the times he had teased her in class, of the way he'd looked at her with such contempt, but Kody didn't show any signs of discomfort. "Nothing?"

"I could try insulting you. Would that help?" Kody grinned.

"Maybe, but don't bother. Then we'd just wind up getting in a fight."

Kody's voice was soft when he spoke again. "Yeah, I'm kind of over being mean to you, anyway."

"And I might accidentally break your leg if you were." Maggie peered at Kody. His hair had shifted away from his face, and now that she was looking at him closely, she could see a deep bruise just beginning to show on his left cheekbone. Maggie lifted her hand from his shoulder to his cheek, her fingers brushing his skin gently. "He did hurt you," she said quietly, almost to herself.

"He deserved what he got," Kody said firmly.

Maggie saw the intensity in his eyes, and she suddenly felt embarrassed standing so close to him. She dropped her hand and her head, breaking away from his gaze. "Let's go sit. I need a break—failing at magic is really tiring." Maggie led the way to the porch while Kody followed slowly, deftly levitating a maple leaf he had scooped off the ground.

"You said there was a long story about the fruit on your front porch," Kody prompted as they settled into the old metal chairs. "Let's hear it."

Maggie told him all of the details, eyeing Kody closely as she talked to see if he gave away any signs of having been behind it. She only felt more reassured that he wasn't, especially when he whistled at the mention of the diamond earrings. "Someone has it bad for you."

"Maybe I should ask my mysterious guardian who left it. I'll bet he saw something." A thought struck Maggie. "How did you wind up seeing the guardian, anyway?"

For the first time, Maggie saw Kody blush. He looked down at his lap, silent. "Kody?"

"I wanted...I came by...I was hoping that you were still up and that I could see you." Kody was still staring down, his fingers restlessly shredding the maple leaf he had been levitating.

"Oh." Maggie wasn't sure what to say, so she finally settled on, "You were going to come to my window?"

"Except I didn't know which window was yours. I didn't exactly plan it out very well. But then I saw that thing standing there, and I got worried. I stuck around to see what would happen."

"What did happen?"

"Nothing. When the sun started to come up, the thing just went." Kody spread his hands. "Like it had invisibility, but I ran straight toward it and didn't hit anything."

"You were at my house all night?"

"I went home after that and got some sleep, but I knew I needed to tell you what had happened."

Maggie wasn't sure if Kody's nocturnal watch made her feel safer or creeped out. Still, a part of her wished he had been on watch Friday night, when he might have seen whoever left the goat. Maggie stood and stretched. "I'm going to get a glass of water. You want anything?"

"No, I'm going to go back out and try some other

things."

When Maggie returned from the kitchen, she didn't
see Kody out by the pond. She walked into the backyard,
scanning for him, then thought to look up. The sky was
empty. Maggie walked a circuit around the house,
calling his name, but Kody wasn't there. She returned to
the house, searching every room in vain, before she
considered that he might be out in the old sunflower
fields. Maggie shouted his name until she was hoarse,
pushing through the withered stalks until she reached the
road. Finally, Maggie had to concede that Kody just
wasn't there anymore. His car was still in the driveway,
but Kody was gone.

Maggie suddenly felt afraid and vulnerable. It was
easy to feel safe with Kody's reassurances, but now that
she was alone, Maggie glanced around her anxiously,
wondering who might be lurking inside the fields or
behind the house. Kody had seemed too concerned about
her safety for Maggie to consider that he might be
playing a joke. Maybe he had flown away so quickly
that he had already been lost to view by the time she
came out of the house. If that was the case, though, then
where could he have gone? And why? Maggie came up
with a list of possibilities, ranging from Kody chasing
off an intruder to him simply flying into town so he
could bring back some fast food. As the minutes ticked
by, though, Maggie began to lose hope in any of her
outlandish theories. She continued to scan above her,
hoping that she would see his black wings against the
blue sky.

If he flew off, Maggie told herself, then he would
have taken his shirt and jacket off first. Maggie looked
around for them, but they were nowhere, and she had to
admit that it was unlikely he had flown anywhere. He
would have heard her shouts if he had simply started
walking, but there was nowhere nearby for him to walk

to in the first place.

Maggie plunged into the sunflower fields again, still determined that she would find Kody somewhere. Visions of mysterious winged creatures standing near her, hidden behind the old stalks, only drove her on.

After making the third lap through the middle of the field closest to the house, Maggie finally gave up. Kody was gone, and although she didn't know why, she was convinced that he hadn't left of his own free will. Someone had grabbed him the moment they were separated.

Maggie screamed Kody's name, feeling her voice vibrate through her body. Every sunflower within a perfect ten-foot radius of her was flattened, pushed out with the force of her emotion. Maggie sat down in the middle of the circle and put her face in her hands, all of her thoughts focused on Kody.

CHAPTER 16

Maggie stayed at the cabin for another two hours, always hoping that Kody would reappear, but always knowing he was gone. Finally, her thoughts turned to how she was going to get home. It was the middle of a Sunday afternoon, so flying was absolutely out of the question. Taking Kody's car was also a bad idea, so Maggie made sure its windows were rolled up, locked the doors, and began walking toward the road, hoping her cell phone would get a signal soon. Maggie was nearly to the road when she got a signal, and she quickly dialed Bree. It went to voicemail. She called Shana next, but got voicemail for her, too. She left messages for both of them. Maggie considered calling her parents, but she didn't want to admit that she had been with Kody. She imagined explaining Kody's disappearance to her dad, and him responding with a gruff, "Good! I hope he doesn't come back." With no other options, Maggie started walking in the direction of downtown Telford.

Maggie looked at every passing car with suspicion, wondering if one of the people speeding past knew what had happened to Kody and whether they were now watching her. By the time she reached the high school, Maggie felt mentally and physically exhausted. She tried calling Bree and Shana again, and Shana picked up on the first ring.

"I was just about to call you back. Sorry, we've been over at my grandma's all afternoon, and Mom makes me keep my phone off when we're there."

"It's okay. Are you free now? I need a ride home."

Maggie could practically see Shana's curious stare through the phone. "Do I need to round up Bree for another epic story?"

"Yeah. But hurry—it's bad."

Maggie paced back and forth while she waited for Shana to arrive. As she made another circuit past the flagpole, her phone rang. It was her mom.

"Where are you?" Wendy said, a note of worry in her voice.

"I'm at the school."

"Your note said you were going to the library."

"I know, Mom. I'm sorry. Shana is bringing me home. I'll—" Maggie was cut short as someone wrested the phone from her hand. Behind her, she heard a deep voice pick up the conversation.

"Mrs. Connolly, this is the Holy and Angelic Reverend Father Colin Buchanan. Your daughter is secure, and I'll personally see to it that she gets home safely."

Maggie whirled around and saw Buchanan, looking as polished as he did on TV, with a crisp olive-green suit and coiffed hair that added at least two inches to his already tall frame. "Come with me, Miss Connolly," he said gravely. "The fate of this world depends on your cooperation."

Maggie just stared at Buchanan, and when he spoke again, his voice was soft. It was, Maggie decided, even more evocative than his shouting on TV. Buchanan had a power about him, and Maggie could almost feel it coiling beneath his calm exterior. "Miss Connolly, you have thrown your lot in with demons. You must repent and turn away from their temptations."

The accusation shocked Maggie into speech. "Are you referring to Kody?"

"Kody, and others."

"First of all," Maggie held up one finger, "Kody is only half-demon. Second, I don't know any other demons. And third, if you know about Kody, then maybe you can tell me what has happened to him."

"You care for him, and you think he cares for you." Buchanan sniffed. "We've done what we thought best."

"What did you do to him?"

"He is safe."

Maggie raised her voice. "Where is he?"

"He is safe, Miss Connolly. And he will continue to be safe as long as you denounce the demons and join forces with us."

Maggie shook her head. "I don't understand. Do you mean you're holding him hostage so I'll…repent or something? Is this how you get people to join your congregation?"

"My congregation? No! My army!" Buchanan's voice began to swell, and he spread his arms wide. "We will defeat the demons once and for all, and after a terrible war, this Earth will know a peace that has not existed since the first days in the Garden of Eden!"

"I'm not joining anyone's army," Maggie said. As much as Buchanan's words confused her, she at least understood that he was behind Kody's disappearance. Realizing she wouldn't win an argument with Buchanan about his supposed army, she changed tactics. "How did you do it? Take Kody, I mean. I walked outside and he was just gone."

"Angels do not rely solely on their wings to move

about this plane," Buchanan said smugly. "They can appear, and disappear, where they wish."

"So you appeared outside the cabin, grabbed Kody, and disappeared with him?"

"Well, I did not. I am only a half-angel, and as such do not possess that great skill. But Ajalon, my lieutenant, executed the plan beautifully."

Maggie frowned. "Did you take Kody off to the angelic plane then, or is he still around here somewhere? And since when do angels kidnap people, anyway?"

"Now, Miss Connolly, I cannot answer all of your questions. And judging by your ignorance about my plans for the future of this world, I believe you are not even asking the most important question of all."

Maggie shrugged, her thoughts still on Kody. "And that is?"

"What you should be asking is, 'Who am I?'" Buchanan smiled widely as Maggie stood straighter, her attention now focused on Buchanan. "Yes, child, I know. The angels saw you and realized that you were the sign they had been waiting more than one-thousand years for, the harbinger of the war that will defeat the demons forever. I will gladly tell you who you are. But you must come with me now." Buchanan gestured to the parking lot, where a gray Cadillac was parked at the curb. A slim man in a black suit was standing next to it.

Maggie hesitated, unsure whether she trusted Buchanan. She wanted answers, yes, but his speech about building an army and defeating the demons sounded like the ravings of a madman. Would she be safe with him? And where was he going to take her anyway? Maggie glanced behind her, looking for an escape route if she decided to run. She jumped when she saw a woman just two feet behind her. She wore a white dress that plunged low in the back, leaving room for huge wings covered in white feathers. Her skin had a pale shimmer to it, and Maggie felt like she couldn't quite focus on the woman. An angel. Another angel, a man this time, silently materialized next to her.

Still undecided, even though she was surrounded, Maggie turned back to Buchanan and asked, "Will you take me to Kody?"

Buchanan sighed. "You will learn to loathe him as we do. But if you agree to help us, then the demon boy will be released. To your care, if that is your desire."

"And what does helping you actually involve?"

"Before I can answer that, I must tell you what you are. We have much to discuss, Miss Connolly. If you please." Buchanan gestured to the Cadillac again, and Maggie sighed. She had no choice, anyway, and whatever she was getting herself into, at least she was about the get the answers that she had been so desperately seeking.

The slim man in the suit opened the back door of the car for Maggie, and just as she began to climb in, Shana pulled into the parking lot. Maggie looked over and saw Shana's mouth drop open when she recognized Buchanan. Shana raised her hands in a questioning gesture while Bree opened the passenger door, and Maggie shook her head. She waved them away, hoping her friends wouldn't follow her into whatever mess she was now embroiled in. When the door of the Cadillac shut behind her, Maggie felt trapped.

Buchanan climbed in next to her while the slim man slid gracefully into the driver's seat. He had the same shimmery appearance as the other angels. As they pulled onto the street, Maggie twisted around in her seat to look for Shana, who was lingering in the parking lot. Maggie ardently wished that she was a medium and could communicate with Shana or Bree.

That thought reminded Maggie that she did have magic she could use. As scared as she was, she knew she should be able to make something happen. Even if she couldn't, Maggie suspected that she would reach a point when her unconscious mind would lash out anyway.

The car had turned onto a road with little traffic, and they were picking up speed. Maggie began to focus, picturing Buchanan telling her that he would release Kody immediately. The preacher remained silent, and Maggie felt her frustration growing. It would be easier to transfer her thoughts if she could touch Buchanan, but the contact would probably rouse his suspicion. She forced herself to keep trying, and finally Buchanan turned to speak to her. Whether her magic was actually working or if he was going to say something else, Maggie never found out. At the same moment, the car lurched forward as something hit them from behind. The startled driver slowed down, and a black SUV pulled up next to them and came over hard into the side of the car. The driver was thrown sideways, and the car skidded off the road into a muddy ditch, coming to a violent stop that threw Maggie against the back of the passenger seat.

The terrible noise and motion had stopped, but Maggie didn't move, too shocked to react yet. Slowly, she began to assess her body, looking for any signs of injury. Her forehead ached from smacking the seat, and Maggie touched the skin there gently. There was no blood. Assured that she was relatively unhurt, Maggie turned toward Buchanan. He was already climbing out of the car. The driver had disappeared entirely. Lucky angel, Maggie thought. I wish I could have disappeared before the crash.

The SUV had stopped, too, and Maggie saw a woman striding toward Buchanan. Maggie gasped when she recognized Healer Waltham.

"You're not taking her anywhere!" Helena shouted.

"Nonsense. You used that demon boy to entice her, but we have him now. She will fight for us."

Helena looked tiny as she stood glaring up at Buchanan, but she held her ground. "You think Maggie will side with anyone who kidnapped her friend? We know what you've done."

"Stop it!" Maggie interjected. "Just stop talking about whose side I'm on and who I'm fighting for. I'm not fighting for anybody. I just want Kody back." Maggie turned to Helena. "And you! I came to your house looking for help, and you acted like I was some kind of a monster. Why won't anyone tell me what's going on?"

Helena bit her lip. "I acted like that because I realized that you were the embodiment of the prophecy. This war is going to happen, and it's my fault for unleashing your power."

Maggie was so frustrated that she couldn't even muster words. She simply screamed. Helena and Buchanan stumbled backwards. "My God, she's powerful," Buchanan said quietly. "Imagine what she will be when she's learned to harness her abilities. The demons are going to die."

"The angels are going to be defeated," Helena corrected.

"Stop talking to each other and tell me what the hell I am." Maggie looked between the two.

"Have you heard of the Morrigan?" Helena asked. Maggie shook her head.

"How about Valkyries?"

"Yes, we learned about them in history. They're from Norse mythology."

"They are now. The Norse called them Valkyries. In Celtic lore, they were blended into one goddess of war and death called Morrigan. Almost every ancient culture has similar mythology about powerful female figures who controlled the outcome of battle. But long before they were mere myths, they were real. The Magistra Mortalis, the mistresses of death. And that, Maggie, is what you are." Helena sounded like a teacher simply giving a history lesson. "The Magistra Mortalis were from this plane, although they were not human, and they were able to work magic on humans, angels, and demons."

Helena paused, and Maggie interjected, "But Kody says I must have demon or angel blood because his magic doesn't work on me."

"Just as angels and demons cannot use magic against each other, neither can they use it against the Magistra Mortalis. I'm sure the demon boy knows nothing of your race. They have all but been forgotten. The Magistra Mortalis would use their magic to help or hinder men in battle, orchestrating it all to secure the victory for the side they had chosen to defend. In school, you were probably taught that Valkyries chose which of the fallen soldiers would be taken to Valhalla, but they were originally thought to choose who fell in battle. That part of the mythology comes from the Magistra Mortalis. They would hurt or even kill those they wished to fail."

"But my parents are human," Maggie said. It was the only thought that was keeping her from screaming again as she tried to absorb the Healer's words.

"Yes, but you must have Magistra Mortalis ancestry." It was Buchanan who had picked up the story. "Many years ago, kings and generals would ask the Magistra Mortalis for help in battle. They would make sacrifices, bring gifts, and even offer up men to be their mates. If a Magistra Mortalis gave birth to a son, it would be human, and it would be given to the father to raise. The daughters they kept to carry on their line. Eventually, the female line diminished as they died out or were killed by warriors who thought they should win or lose battles on their own merit. But those human sons lived on, carrying the DNA deep within them. It was prophesied that someday, a Magistra Mortalis would be born again, and that with her help, the war between angels and demons would be fought. The side she chose to support would be victorious. You fulfilled that prophecy."

"Demons and angels have always fought."

"Yes, but on our own plane. This war will determine which of us will reign over Earth." Helena sounded confident, as if the victor had already been determined.

"When you say 'us,'" Maggie prompted.

Helena nodded. "I took the form of a human because I liked being on this plane, and I liked helping people. Demons aren't what you've been made to believe, Maggie, though I meant it when I told you to keep an eye on Kody. He is powerful, though not as powerful as you. You have the upper hand with him. Remember that."

The distant sound of a siren made Maggie's response die on her lips, and Buchanan grabbed her arm. "Someone must have called 911 for us. How kind."

Helena took Maggie's other arm. "Your car is in a ditch. Maggie will come with me."

"We'll go together," Maggie said firmly, wrenching her arms free. "You both owe me more answers."

Maggie insisted on being taken straight home as she climbed into the back seat of Helena's SUV. When Helena protested her demand, Maggie raised her hands as if she was warding herself against the Healer's words. A warmth spread through Maggie, and she felt a strange vibration, like a tingling on her skin. *There it is*, she thought. *If I can feel my magic like this, then I'm getting closer to learning how to control it.*

Buchanan and Helena seemed to sense the power Maggie radiated. Helena relented and let Maggie give directions to her house while Buchanan sat back moodily in the passenger seat, his attention focused on texting as he tried to ignore Helena's presence. Maggie dreaded the confrontation with her parents. How much of this did they know? Had they been hiding all of this from her since she was born?

During the drive, Maggie said, "Healer Waltham? If demons aren't what I think they are, then what are they? I thought they were evil, the opposite of angels."

Helena laughed darkly. "Evil? Sometimes. Millennia ago, a group of angels rebelled against God. It's not that they wanted to be bad; they simply wished to be autonomous, unaccountable to anyone but themselves. Angels live under the rules set by their God; demons have free will. Because of that, some demons have no qualms about wreaking havoc on this plane. There are good and bad beings on both sides." Helena made a point of turning to scowl at Buchanan.

"Despicable creatures," Buchanan said casually, as if it was a debate he held often. "Rules are what make societies function, the threads that create order out of chaos."

"Semantics." Helena shrugged.

In the silence that followed, Maggie closed her eyes. She had so much information to absorb, but still so many questions. The two most important questions that kept running through her head were "Why me?" and "Is Kody okay?" He had tricked her into having her spell removed, and she had endured his bullying for years, but Maggie felt like he was being unfairly punished. His intention in getting her to see Healer Waltham in the first place had been selfish, but she knew he had never intended any harm to come to either of them. And now, Maggie thought, there's going to be a war that will affect everyone on this planet. The idea was too much for her to envision, so she simply focused on the present. She had to get away from Buchanan and Helena. From there, Maggie simply needed to get Kody back and find a way to prevent the war from happening.

Maggie almost laughed at the absurdity of the

situation. She could feel the vibration around her heighten, creating what felt like a protective barrier around her. She feared what might happen if her distress continued to grow. She had broken Jeff's leg without ever feeling a buildup of power like this, and Maggie suddenly understood how someone like her could affect a battle. If she were to focus that power and direct it at one person, Maggie knew she could kill. It wouldn't be a slow process or take effort like turning the grass brown at the cabin. It would be swift and merciless.

Angels govern themselves by rules that God made, Maggie thought. Demons have no rules. "What are my rules?" she mused out loud.

"Choose your side based on your own moral beliefs of who is right and who is wrong," Buchanan said.

"Or choose based on the side that gives you the greatest honor," added Helena.

Maggie's eyes narrowed. "You mentioned before that armies would make sacrifices to the Valkyries. Er," Maggie tried to remember the Latin name, "the Magistra Mortalis. All those gifts on my doorstep last weekend, those were bribes?"

"Yes, from the angels." Buchanan sounded pleased with himself.

"I thought someone was playing a joke." Maggie looked at Buchanan, her tone sarcastic. "You should have left a note so I knew who they were from."

"We had underestimated your ignorance of the situation. By the way, I do feel that I should apologize about the goat. One of our soldiers took a rather Old Testament approach to your offerings."

"You thought that leaving me flowers and diamond earrings would make me kill demons for you?" Maggie shook her head, disgusted to think that she came from a line of creatures whose loyalty could be so easily purchased.

"We wanted you to see that we would be loyal to you, and that, in turn, you would receive accolades for your loyalty to us." Buchanan pronounced the words grandly, as if he expected Maggie to begin thanking him profusely for the presents.

Maggie ignored Buchanan, instead directing Helena. The Healer turned the SUV onto Maggie's street and braked abruptly. "Oh," was all she said.

The war really had begun, and a battle was taking place in front of Maggie's house. A line of angels were standing shoulder-to-shoulder in the front yard, facing half a dozen demons who were advancing toward the front door. They all carried an assortment of swords, knives, and spears, and already one angel was sprawled on the ground, a streak of red marring his white wings.

Buchanan didn't seem surprised, and he said with confidence, "Now, Maggie, it's time for you to choose a side. The victor is up to you."

CHAPTER 17

"You set this up." Maggie's voice was directed at Buchanan, but she was still staring out of the windshield at the odd scene.

"I sent Ajalon here to arrange your first test."

"Ajalon. Your lieutenant." Maggie put emphasis on the last word, her disgust clear. Buchanan made a noncommittal noise and opened the car door, motioning for Maggie to follow.

Maggie climbed out of the back seat in time to watch an angel drive a spear into a demon's shoulder. She winced at the sight of the dark blood that poured from the wound as the demon howled in a mixture of pain and rage. She wanted to look away, but Maggie stood, transfixed. She had never seen a full-blooded demon before, and she couldn't blame Healer Waltham for taking the form of a human. Like Kody, the demons had black sinewy wings. Their bodies seemed basically human, but where the angels had a glow about them, the demons had a dark shimmer, a constantly-shifting shadow that enveloped them. Rather than making her eyes feel unfocused, like the effect the angels had on her,

Maggie felt as if she was trying to see something in the dark. She could sense the shape of the demon beneath the shadow, but she couldn't discern where the dark ended and their skin began.

"Healer Waltham, walk around to the back door. Get my parents out and take them somewhere safe." The fear she felt for her parents' safety had to be nothing compared to the terror they must be feeling now.

"We can do that," Buchanan said quickly.

"I asked Healer Waltham to do it." Helena was already skirting the battle, making her way behind the house. "You thought that putting my parents in danger would make me fight for your side? First Kody and now this?"

Buchanan remained silent for a long moment, carefully considering his words. "We are at war. The future peace of this world depends on you supporting us. I know our methods may seem odd to you, but in the end, you will understand that it is for the best."

Another angel fell to the ground, a demon's sword embedded in its chest. Maggie covered her mouth with her hands, forcing back a scream of horror. "Choose the victor," Buchanan said again.

"No. This is not my war."

"You must choose."

"Or else what? You'll just keep preaching at me? You'll threaten more of the people that I care about? I might be your stupid prophecy, but that doesn't mean I have to be a part of this."

"You cannot stand by and do nothing. Even if you do not consciously choose, you will determine the outcome of this war. You can run away, hide from all of us, but your unconscious mind will make a choice, and the battle will fall as you see fit. You cannot escape now that you are a part of it."

"That's not fair!" Maggie shouted. She felt the

energy around her pulse, growing outward before contracting again. If Buchanan keeps going, she thought, he'll be the first person I kill. Maggie turned away from Buchanan and the battle, breathing slowly. Willing herself to calm down, she stared at the sky, wishing she could just fly away and hide. The sounds of the battle behind her—the clang of swords and spears clashing and the shouts of the soldiers—faded.

Maggie became aware that she hadn't simply pushed the noise out of her mind. The battle had ceased. Slowly, she turned around, wondering if her unconscious mind really had picked a side and it was already over.

Three demons and four angels were still standing, but their weapons were lowered, hanging loosely from their hands. They were all staring at Maggie. As one, the seven soldiers bowed their heads in reverence.

One of the angels, whom Maggie assumed was Ajalon, raised his head. "Defeat the demons for our Magistra Mortalis!" He lifted his sword and swung it at the nearest demon, who deftly parried the attack with a spear.

Maggie began to whisper to herself, "I will not choose."

Buchanan, watching her, started to fidget, sweat beading on his forehead. "They fight for you," he implored.

"You fight for yourselves. I will not choose."

"You must choose!" Buchanan, who had spoken so authoritatively since they met, now sounded anxious. The battle continued, though neither side was able to make progress, and Buchanan began to turn his head from the battle to Maggie, who was still repeating her words quietly. "You *will* choose," he said in an undertone. "Ajalon! It is time," he called out.

Ajalon disappeared immediately, and a demon's knife sliced through the space where the angel's arm had been. Suspecting a trick, the demon paused, legs bent as if preparing to pounce. Ajalon reappeared in the same spot, and the demon lunged, knife raised.

The demon's knife plunged into Kody, whose body was being held like a shield by Ajalon.

Maggie screamed and the demon fell backwards, howling. He dropped the knife and clutched his hand. "It burns!"

"Very good," Buchanan said quietly, a slow smile spreading across his face.

"Get away from him!" Maggie shouted. The demons recoiled at the words, and Maggie felt another pulse of the energy around her. This time, it was like a shockwave that crashed into the three demons, sending them sprawling. Instantly, the angels rushed forward, more energy in their attack.

"She fights for us!" Buchanan said triumphantly. He raised his hands in a gesture Maggie had seen him do in the video she had watched, when he had been addressing his congregation. Now, he was addressing his army.

Maggie's own voice was soft when she spoke. "I fight for Kody." Without thinking of her own danger, Maggie ran forward into the battle. Instinctively, she flung one arm out, her palm raised toward an angel who was lunging at an already-injured demon. The angel fell backwards. The other two who were attacking the remaining demons stopped short, hesitating as they realized that Maggie was not helping them. She stalked right in front of them, forcing them to back away from the demons.

As she closed in on Ajalon, Maggie could feel the anticipation from the soldiers behind her. The battle had paused again, this time not out of reverence for Maggie, but out of fear.

Ajalon still had Kody in a tight grip. Kody was slumped against Ajalon, blood pouring from the knife wound in his side. Maggie felt sick at the sight of so much blood, but she forced herself to focus. Again, she raised her arm, this time toward Ajalon.

Ajalon swung around so that Kody's body was between them. Kody looked nearly unconscious, his eyes half-closed and his face ashen. He winced as Ajalon's fingers tightened around his neck.

"You will kill this boy if you advance against me!" Ajalon raised his sword, indicating that he would kill Kody himself if Maggie tried to fight him.

Maggie lowered her arm slowly and stood quietly, staring at Ajalon. He took her stillness as a sign of resignation, and he lifted his eyes to the sky. "Our Father will be pleased with your decision," he said. "You will lead us into war, and we will know no fear with you watching over us."

Still Maggie was silent. She knew she was losing precious time: Kody was bleeding profusely and the battle behind her might resume at any moment. She was focusing her energy again, preparing not just for another strike but for an escape. Maggie knew she couldn't hide from them for long, but she at least needed time to think, without Buchanan or anyone else trying to persuade her.

Slowly, Maggie unbuttoned her flannel shirt and took it off. She had started wearing a tank top under every outfit, just in case she wanted—or needed—to fly. Maggie whispered, "Manifestum alae," and her wings appeared. She could hear the gasp of the angels and demons behind her.

Ajalon nodded encouragingly. "Yes, that's it. Unleash all of your power and this war will be over quickly. Let us finish this first battle now."

Maggie raised her arm again, aiming her hand not at Ajalon but at his sword. With a cry of pain, Ajalon dropped it. Maggie rushed forward, scooping up the sword as she skirted around Ajalon. He froze as she held the point of the sword against his back. "Let him go and this battle *will* end," she said firmly.

Ajalon complied, slowly loosening his grip on Kody, who slid down to the ground and lay still. Maggie's heart beat wildly as she saw his pallid face, worrying that he had already bled to death. The fear and anger finally became too much, and Maggie knew she was going to lose what little control she had gained over her magic. Her brain screamed at her to reel in her emotions, but it was too late. Another shockwave of power radiated from her body.

Ajalon, another angel and one of the demons stiffened as the power hit them, all three standing tall and rigid for a few seconds before crashing straight forward. Ajalon fell onto his face, hitting the ground hard beside Kody. He didn't move. Maggie looked up and saw the horrified look on Buchanan's face. His mouth was stuck open after crying, "No!"

Maggie sidestepped Ajalon's prone body and bent down over Kody. She still wasn't sure he was alive, but she scooped him up in her arms and stood, tottering under his weight. She shifted him so that she had better balance, then ran forward as fast as she could. Maggie ran out of her yard and into the street before her wings finally carried her upward. She beat them as hard as she could, fighting to gain altitude. She knew she wouldn't be able to fly very far, and she hoped that no one would follow her. If she could buy herself even just a few minutes, she might be able to begin processing everything she had learned, seen, and done in the past hour.

By the time she reached Blue Fern Park, Maggie could already feel her wings aching under the strain of carrying Kody. She flew down to a small clearing in a heavily wooded area on the far side of the park. She briefly wondered how many neighbors had witnessed the battle and her flight.

Maggie hit the ground hard, falling to her knees and dropping Kody onto the ground. He groaned and Maggie leaned over him, relieved that he was still alive. He slowly opened his eyes. "You're bleeding," he said softly.

Kody's eyes were fixed on Maggie's tank top, which was covered in his own blood. "No, I'm fine," Maggie reassured him. "And I'm going to help you."

Maggie reached into her pocket, searching for her cell phone so she could call an ambulance. It wasn't there. She checked the other pocket of her jeans, then swore as she realized that her phone was inside her purse, and that was still in Healer Waltham's SUV.

In her frustration, Maggie slammed her hands on the ground, curling her fingers around the grass. The feel of the dry blades made her think of the grass at the cabin, and she looked back at Kody. His eyes had closed again, and Maggie knew there was no time to waste. If she could make something die, then there was just the slightest chance she could heal, too.

Did I make Ajalon die? Maggie pushed the thought out of her mind. I can worry about that later, she thought.

Maggie bent over Kody, putting her hands against his chest. His shallow breathing felt tired and weak under her fingers. Maggie's forehead creased as she closed her eyes, building an image of Kody in her mind. She saw his side, the skin whole and healthy, the wound having closed itself on the outside and mended itself on the inside. Once she had the image clear in her mind, Maggie sent it down her arms and into Kody's body. She felt a tingling sensation build in her hands, and Maggie's confidence surged. She put all of her energy into her task, until her mental image of a healed Kody faded and turned black.

Chapter 18

"Maggie, please! Wake up!"

The voice sounded far away. Maggie felt her body rocking back and forth, like she was on a boat. It's that dream again, she thought. I'm back on that boat in the sea of blood. With an effort, Maggie opened her eyes and found herself staring into a pair of black ones. Kody sat back, relief showing on his face. "Finally," he said.

Maggie felt heavy, and she struggled to sit up. The sun had already sunk below the horizon, and she shivered in the chilly twilight air. Kody was still more pale than usual, but he was conscious and sitting up. "It worked?" Maggie asked.

In response, Kody lifted his shirt. There was a red line on his side, but it looked more like a scratch or a mostly-healed cut than the wide gash it had been. "You mostly got it before you decided to take another nap."

"Did I pass out?"

Kody nodded. "I think you used up all of your energy."

"I'm sorry they did this to you. It's my fault."

Kody gave a nonchalant shrug. "Technically, it's my

fault. I'm the one who talked you into undoing any spells on you. What are you, anyway? The angels were talking about you like you're some kind of war hero."

"I have a lot to tell you, but not here. I'm hungry. And cold."

Kody moved closer to Maggie and wrapped his arms around her. She leaned against him, relishing the warmth of his embrace. "The angels also think I was part of some plan to make you sympathetic to the demons," he said.

"Yeah. Hey, did you know that Healer Waltham is a demon? Full-blooded."

"No way. Really? She always acted like I was some kind of terror. Takes one to know one, I guess."

"She said you're very powerful."

Kody rested his chin on top of Maggie's head. "If I was, I could have fought off the angel who took me. I can't believe he used me against the demon like that. Jerk."

"He did it because Buchanan thought that if the angels threatened to hurt you, I'd relent and fight for them to keep you safe."

"Fight for them? And who's Buchanan?"

"Like I said, we've got a lot of catching up to do. The question is, where can we go? They're probably watching us right now."

"Then I'm taking you home," Kody said firmly. "There is nowhere we can go that they can't find us. If they're going to attack, then there's nothing we can do about it. Until then, you need rest, and we both need a shower."

"And I want to make sure my parents are okay." Maggie sighed, reluctant to pull away from Kody. It was the first time since he'd disappeared earlier in the day that she had felt any kind of peace.

Apparently, Kody felt the same way because he made

no move to stand. "You know how I asked you at The Roundhouse if you were scared?"

"Yes."

"I'm scared, too." Kody's voice was barely above a whisper, and Maggie hugged him tighter.

After a long moment, Kody stood and offered his hand to Maggie. As he pulled her to her feet, he said, "Do you want to walk or fly?"

"Walk. I don't think I have the energy to fly."

"Then you should put your wings away. We don't want to attract too much attention."

Maggie complied, and as she turned to walk with Kody, he reached over and took her hand. Maggie began to tell him everything that had happened that afternoon, and Kody took the news about her being a Magistra Mortalis easier than she had expected. "And here I thought you had demon or angel blood. So much for my 'I told you so,'" was his casual response.

They reached the doorstep of Maggie's house just as she finished telling Kody about her flight to the park. She turned the doorknob, but it was locked and her key was in her purse. "I can fly, but I can't even get into my own house," she intoned. Maggie rang the doorbell and waited, worried that her parents wouldn't be there and also worried that they would be. Telling them everything was going to be difficult.

The porch lights began to flicker, and Kody glanced at Maggie. "Hey," he said, squeezing her hand, "it's going to be okay. I'll stay with you no matter what happens."

The lights returned to their steady brightness as Maggie managed a small laugh. "I'm not sure that helps. My parents don't exactly approve of you."

The door opened, and Maggie was relieved to see her parents, both unharmed. Her mom rushed out and threw her arms around Maggie, crying her name over and over.

Wendy finally released Maggie, ushering her inside. Richard hugged her, also, although he remained calm. When he released Maggie, she looked past him and saw Bree and Shana huddled together on the couch.

"What are you two doing here?"

It was Richard who answered. "They came straight here this afternoon, after they saw you leave the high school with Buchanan. Sit down, Maggie. We have a lot to discuss."

Maggie and Kody both squeezed onto the couch next to Bree and Shana. Bree yelped. "You're both hurt!"

"It's Kody's blood," Maggie answered at the same time Kody said, "Maggie healed me."

"Maggie healed you?" Richard was staring at Kody, who turned to look at Maggie, as if asking for her permission to explain.

"You really do have strong magic," Wendy said. She sighed and sat down. "Honey, we didn't know. We thought...when you were born..." As Wendy searched for the right words, Richard walked over and put a supportive hand on her shoulder. "The doctor said the wings were just a weird anomaly, some defect in your DNA."

"We had your wings removed magically, hidden," Richard took up the story, "but you were already manifesting magic by the time you were two years old. Not just one Talent, but several. We didn't know what was happening, but we were afraid you might hurt yourself or others. We had a Healer put a spell on you to bind your magic."

Maggie gasped. "You did lie to me! You kept telling me I would manifest a Talent someday, when you knew I wouldn't!"

Wendy held up a hand. "No, it wasn't like that. The spell was supposed to be temporary. It was supposed to last ten years or so, no more than that. So when you got to be a teenager and no Talent had manifested yet, we kept hoping that some event would trigger the re-manifestation of your magic."

"At the beginning of the school year, your mom and I agreed that if you hadn't manifested a Talent by your eighteenth birthday, then we would take you to a Healer ourselves. As we now know, Kody beat us to that." Richard glared at Kody, who was smart enough to look chastised, through Maggie knew otherwise.

"We really didn't know what you were, Maggie," Wendy continued. "On Friday, I got a phone call from Colin Buchanan. He told me that you were the fulfillment of a prophecy and that you were going to be pivotal in a war. I laughed, thinking it was some ploy to get donations, and hung up on him. He called the house a dozen times after that, but I wouldn't answer. And then today, that war began in our front yard."

"Buchanan set it up. He wants me to fight for the angels in their war against the demons." Maggie could hear the resignation in her voice.

"Healer Waltham told us everything. She got us, even Bree and Shana, out of the house safely and assured us that you would be okay. You are okay, aren't you?" Wendy looked at Maggie expectantly.

"I'm hungry and tired. And I'd like to put on some clean clothes." Maggie turned to Bree and Shana. "So I guess you two are filled in on what I am, and what I'm supposed to do?"

"We got the whole story," Shana assured her.

"I'm kind of disappointed. I finally find out what I am, and everybody else knows before I can tell them. Well, I had the satisfaction of telling Kody, at least."

Bree leaned forward so she could get a good look at Kody. "What did you mean when you said Maggie healed you?"

Kody briefly described what had happened with the

angels and his injury in the battle. He looked proudly at Maggie when he concluded with a description of her magical healing, but her parents looked more worried than impressed.

"None of us are safe," Richard said gravely. "If the angels are willing to use Kody as leverage, then they might be willing to use any of us. Bree, Shana, now that you girls know Maggie is okay, you need to go home. Don't go anywhere alone, and don't talk to anyone you don't know. Go to school tomorrow, then go straight home afterward. Do you understand me?"

Both girls acknowledged him nervously. They hugged Maggie, whispered words of encouragement to her, then left.

"Kody, you need to head home, too," Richard continued. "Do you need a ride?"

"No," Maggie said. "Kody stays here."

"I'm sure his mother is worried about him," Wendy began.

"If the angels want to kidnap him again, then they're going to do it wherever he is. He's safer here with me." Maggie's voice was firm.

"Fine," Richard conceded. "Kody, call your mother and ask her to bring you some fresh clothes. We'll take you to school in the morning."

"School?" Maggie couldn't imagine actually going to her classes with everything else that was going on.

"Yes, school," Wendy said. "You'll probably be safest there, among all the other students. As long as no one is dying in our front yard, then we are going to carry on as normally as possible."

"How many angels and demons died today?" Maggie asked quietly.

"When we got back here, the front yard was empty," Richard said.

Maggie still didn't know whether she had killed

Ajalon and the others. She told herself again not to think about it. After all, she doubted that angels were easy to kill. She tried to forget the entire battle as she stood under the hot water of a shower later, but she was sure that she would never get the images of so much blood and violence out of her mind.

Kody's mom had stopped by while Maggie was showering, and Kody said she had been anticipating his call. Healer Waltham had paid her a visit after she had seen Maggie's parents to safety, revealing herself as a demon and explaining the danger that Kody was in. Apparently, the news gave Kody's mom an instant dislike of Maggie until Kody told her that she had saved his life.

Once both Maggie and Kody were showered and in clean clothes, they sat down for a somber dinner with Wendy and Richard. Wendy announced her plan to have Maggie's great-aunt Sarah keep watch on the house throughout the night.

Maggie wondered if her mysterious guardian would be at her window again, but she never got the opportunity to find out. She was so exhausted that she was asleep just seconds after settling into bed, and she slept quietly the entire night.

It felt strange to be dropped off at school the next morning with Kody, and Maggie realized as soon as they stepped out of the car that her parents and friends weren't the only ones who had heard the news about her. Students actually stopped when they saw Maggie, and some pointed at her as they spoke behind their hands to each other.

"So I guess a few people saw what happened yesterday," Kody began. He looked anxiously at Maggie. "Are you going to be able to hold it together?"

"I have to. I can't hurt anyone else."

"I'll walk you to your homeroom." Kody could sense

Maggie's unease, and he took her hand. Instantly, Maggie felt calmer. Maggie said as much to Kody, who smirked. "Maybe I can work some magic on you, after all," he said.

Students continued to stare at Maggie as they walked, and Maggie wondered how many of them knew about the battle and her role in it, and how many of them were simply shocked to see her walking hand-in-hand with Kody. At the front door of her homeroom classroom, Kody said, "Good luck," and left. The hallway lights dimmed as he walked away, and Kody glanced over his shoulder, giving Maggie a reassuring wink.

By the time first period was over, Maggie had decided that the stares were at least less traumatizing than the teasing she used to endure. Now, students weren't looking at her mockingly. Instead, they seemed to be slightly in awe of her. No one said a word to her until Readers class, when Mrs. Simmons stopped at her desk while handing back graded homework. "I'm surprised you came to school today," she said.

"Me, too. My parents thought it was best."

When Mrs. Simmons spoke again, her voice had dropped so low that only Maggie could hear her. "I have a cousin whose father was an angel. Buchanan tried to recruit him to his cause a few years ago, promising that the angels would win when the war finally began. He refused, calling the prophecy nonsense." Mrs. Simmons paused, considering her next words. "Buchanan is...unstable. Be wary of him, despite his angelic parentage."

Maggie laughed tonelessly. "Don't I know it."

"Just be careful, okay, Maggie? Don't take sides until you've weighed the consequences."

Mrs. Simmons walked away, and shortly thereafter called the class to attention. She announced that they were finished studying Tarot and would turn their attention to astrology. Maggie had already pulled her Tarot deck out and placed it on her desk. She idly began to flip through the cards until she came to the Knight of Swords, the one that looked so much like her. Her mind flashed back to her standoff with Ajalon, when she had held the sword to his back. She ran her fingers over the face of the card, remembering how sure her arm had felt with her fingers curled around the hilt. It had felt so natural, so right, that Maggie hadn't found the sword cumbersome at all.

Maggie's eyes refocused on the card, and she began to look at the wand in the Knight's left hand. An indicator of magic. It seemed odd that the Knight of Swords and the Knight of Wands should be holding both tokens. The card that resembled Kody was underneath what Maggie thought of as her card, and she set the two of them side-by-side. She began to go through the rest of the deck, looking for another card that bore more than its signature token—a wand, cup, pentacle or sword—but none did.

Maggie flipped one card over and looked at the back, where a black filigree design was stamped. She had never looked closely at this side, and she realized the filigree had words cleverly woven into it. One word said "divination" and another "prophecies." I am a prophecy, she thought, so how perfect that I'm in this deck.

The words continued to pull at her thoughts, and Maggie lingered after class to talk to Mrs. Simmons. She held out the deck, backside up. "What do you know about this deck?" Maggie began.

"Ah, the Prophecy Deck," her teacher said fondly. "I didn't realize this was the deck you had chosen from the cabinet. How fitting."

"Why is it called the Prophecy Deck?"

"A lot of decks have a theme. Some decks might use popular book characters or mythological creatures in their illustrations. All of these illustrations are based on prophecies. The artist was a powerful Reader. He didn't know the actual prophecies in many cases, but he could see images of the people around whom each prophecy was told. I only recognize a few of the prophecies in this deck myself."

Maggie held up the Knight of Swords. "That's me."

"So it is. As I said, it's fitting that you wound up with this deck. It would seem that the artist saw you quite clearly in his mind."

Maggie then held up the Knight of Wands. "This is Kody Brandt."

Mrs. Simmons's eyes widened in surprise. "You recognize the image? Are you sure?"

"It looks just like him, and look how similar it is to my card, like we're linked. But that would mean Kody is the fulfillment of a prophecy, too."

"I don't know what that prophecy would be, if it really is a friend of yours represented here. I don't know about anyone linked to your own story. Like I said, many of these prophecies are obscure. I wouldn't have heard about the prophecy of the Magistra Mortalis if it weren't for my cousin and his talks with Buchanan."

Maggie was unsatisfied with Mrs. Simmons's answers because all it did was raise more questions. How did Kody figure into a deck of prophecy cards? And if he was tied to a prophecy, then what was it, and did it have anything to do with her?

CHAPTER 19

Kody was already waiting at Maggie's usual lunch table when she got there. Bree and Shana looked resigned to having him present, and Bree was at least attempting to be friendly to him, asking him how he'd slept on the Connollys' couch. Kody gave Bree a curt answer, but Maggie could see that he wasn't trying to be rude; the way he kept running his hand through his hair showed how on edge he was.

"What?" was all Maggie said as she dropped her backpack on the ground.

"Someone came into Naturals looking for me," Kody said. "This lady, who told Mr. Frasier that she was a grief counselor and needed to see me. Mr. Frasier told her no because he didn't know her, but she kept insisting. I thought she was going to attack him she got so mad."

"Was she an angel or a demon?" Shana had risen from her seat, listening to Kody but looking around at the tables near them, suddenly suspicious of everyone.

"I don't know. She could have been human for all I know. Mr. Frasier finally got her out of there."

Bree was looking uneasy now, too. "What did she want with you? Do they want to take you hostage again?"

"Kody, I'm not sure that the angels kidnapped you just to get at me," Maggie began. She gestured for Shana to sit down, and she laid the two Tarot cards in the middle of the table.

Bree gasped and Shana swore, but Kody said, "I don't get it. Why do these look like us?"

Maggie briefly explained the significance of the deck, and Kody's eyes narrowed as she suggested that he might be linked to a prophecy, too. "If I was linked to you through some kind of prophecy, I think we would know about it by now," he said slowly. "The angel who took me—that Ajalon guy—said you were demanding to have me returned, and that Buchanan had promised he'd let me go if you joined them. Ajalon said he was happy to let me die, promise or no promise. I'd think they would want me alive if I was tied to all of this."

"Surely they wouldn't kill you." Maggie was frowning.

"I'm pretty sure I was supposed to die yesterday. Ajalon wanted that demon to kill me."

The table fell quiet, and Maggie glanced at the students around them, talking and laughing and eating their lunches. How nice it must be, she thought, to be so oblivious to everything that's happening. Whether she chose a side or not, the war would affect every one of her classmates. It had been impossible to envision the outcome of the war on a worldwide scale, but sitting there looking at the people she had known her whole life, Maggie could appreciate the impact every decision she made could have. If she sided with the angels, they might all be forced to follow a new set of rules, a new regime headed, she had no doubt, by Buchanan himself. But if she helped the demons win, what kind of chaos would ensue?

Vaguely, Maggie realized that Bree was talking. "We'll call her. It's our best bet," she was saying. Bree was already standing, pulling her backpack over her shoulder and gathering up her uneaten lunch. "Come on, let's go to the library. I feel like we're being watched out here."

Maggie trailed after Bree, Shana and Kody, feeling strangely detached from everything and everyone around her. Students were still staring and occasionally pointing at her, but Maggie barely noticed. Her head was too full of questions and the weight of the responsibilities that had been laid on her to worry about petty gossip.

Bree headed straight for a computer once they were in the library. She looked up the phone number for Healer Waltham's office and called on her cell phone. When Helena picked up, Bree didn't even bother to introduce herself. "We need to know what the prophecy is about Kody," she said. There was a pause, and then Bree continued with, "Oh, I'm a friend of Maggie's. She found something...oh, here, you can talk to her." Bree handed the phone over, and Maggie picked up the conversation, retelling her story about the Tarot cards.

Helena hesitated, though it was clear that she knew something. When she finally gave an answer, it still wasn't enough for Maggie. "I'm sorry, but I don't know much. They say that it's dangerous for you and the demon boy to be together, but I don't know any details. Buchanan would probably know."

Maggie grimaced. "Thanks, but he and I aren't on speaking terms at the moment."

"It could mean that you and Kody are dangerous together, a formidable team," Helena warned, "but it could also mean that you are dangerous to each other. Be on your guard, both of you."

Maggie gave Bree her phone back, reluctantly

relaying the information. Kody looked nonplussed, but he remained silent. "I don't like this," Shana said. "Kody has someone trying to come after him at school, there's something about the two of you that is really bad, but we don't know who it's bad for or how, and at some point both sides are going to force you to make a choice, Maggie."

Maggie slumped down into a chair. She spread her hands. "But what can I do?"

"Keep practicing your magic," Kody suggested. "You need to learn how to protect yourself. Angels and demons can't use magic against you, but they can find other ways of hurting you or forcing you to do what they want."

"Like hurting my friends, or using magic against them," Maggie said, looking apologetically at Kody.

"We're going to practice after school." Kody turned to Bree and Shana. "You two should practice, too."

They all agreed to go to Maggie's house after school because she knew there was no chance that her parents would let her go elsewhere. Her dad had insisted on picking her up at school, so Shana rode with them while Bree drove Kody to his grandfather's cabin to retrieve his Camaro.

Maggie filled Richard in on the day's events as they drove, Shana interjecting details from the back seat. Maggie was determined to have no more secrets between herself and her parents. He was surprised about Kody being a prophecy, too, but he tried to downplay it. "I'm sure Buchanan would have told us if it was important," he said, feigning more serenity than he felt on the subject.

Shana and Maggie looked online for information about prophecies while they waited for Bree and Kody to arrive. They were unable to find much that was specific, and even putting in the search term "Magistra

Mortalis"—now that Maggie knew what she was—yielded no results. Maggie really was descended from an obscure race, and only the angels and demons had cared to keep their memory alive because of the prophecy.

"I guess we do need to talk to an angel or a demon," Maggie finally conceded, "but I am not going near Buchanan." She got up from her desk and collapsed onto her bed, where Shana was already sprawled on her back, staring at the ceiling.

"I'm surprised he hasn't come near you. It's been a full day since you've seen him. What gives?" Shana asked.

"He'd rather sneak around and spy on us than approach us directly, probably so he can find new ways to get you to join the angels," Bree said. She and Kody had just walked into Maggie's room. Despite Bree's ominous statement, Maggie was glad to see the relaxed manner between her and Kody. Clearly, Bree and Shana were developing some regard for Kody. Maggie could appreciate just how hard it was to get over years of prejudice against him.

"A car followed us out to the cabin," Bree continued. "We were afraid to pull into the drive because they could trap us there, so we ditched the idea of getting Kody's car and came here."

"Did you see who was driving?" Maggie sat up.

"My friend the grief counselor, the woman who came into Naturals. We got a good look at her when we turned around." Kody frowned. "If she follows us here…"

"They already know where we are," Maggie interrupted. "I'm sure they knew exactly where we were in the park last night, too. But they're holding back for some reason."

"You took out Mister Big, Bad and Feathery yesterday," Kody reminded her. "I don't think that was part of their plan. They're regrouping."

"Then we should be doing the same. What are we going to practice first?"

Kody wound up being the unexpected leader of the practice session, instructing Shana to work on not just levitating objects but on moving them quickly so she could throw objects at anyone who might attack her. The four of them had to go outside into the back yard when Shana got overly eager and sent a pencil flying so hard that it embedded itself in the wall.

Bree was already incredibly good at her invisibility, and she could turn invisible almost instantly. Instead of practicing her own Talent, she became the target of Maggie's magic. At Kody's insistence, Maggie worked on her small ability to plant a thought in someone's mind. It continued to take a lot of concentration, but with Kody's guidance, she soon had Bree unwittingly reciting the ABC's in a singsong voice. When Maggie started laughing, the magical connection was broken and Bree stopped abruptly. "I can't believe I'm letting you do this to me," she said. "I have to say though, you're getting really good. I'm proud of you, Mags."

The afternoon wore on, and Maggie was so pleased with her progress that she forgot, for a short while, the whole reason she was having to work so hard on her magic. It wasn't until Wendy came outside to call them in that Maggie was reminded of everything outside her circle of friends. Wendy's face was strained, and she looked worriedly at Kody. "Your mom is here," she said. Something about her voice alarmed Kody, and he sprinted inside the house. By the time the rest of them filed into the living room, Kody was looking intently at his mother as she spoke rapidly, her hands flying in gestures of distress.

"What happened?" Maggie asked her mom quietly.

"I wasn't able to get the whole story. She wanted to see Kody and know he was safe before telling me anything." Wendy paused, watching the scene in front of her. "She seems to love him very much."

"Of course she does. He's not awful, Mom." Maggie paused before adding, "And he's been really nice to me lately. I don't think I would have made it to homeroom this morning if it wasn't for him."

Kody's mom had obviously finished with her story because her hands finally stopped moving and settled onto Kody's shoulders. "I'm just glad you're still safe," Maggie heard her say.

Kody turned to the others. "Buchanan paid her a visit today, and he said that he'll hurt her if I don't stop hanging out with Maggie."

"Mrs. Brandt?" Maggie's voice sounded small. "Do you know the prophecy about Kody?"

"Call me Ellen. And no, I have no idea what you're talking about. I thought you were the prophecy?"

For the fourth time that day, Maggie related the news about the Tarot cards that looked like them. Ellen could only shake her head, although she was obviously unnerved by the news. "I've never heard anything about a prophecy."

"Buchanan is going to great lengths to separate you and Kody," Richard spoke up. "Again, he's risking turning Maggie against the angels just to keep her and Kody separated. I don't like it. We need to know why he doesn't want them together."

"Especially since Kody can't do magic on me," Maggie added.

"Why would you say that?" Ellen asked.

"Because he's tried, and nothing happens. Angel and demon magic won't work on the Magistra Mortalis."

"But Kody has human magic, too. It could be that he just hasn't tried the right kind of magic on you."

Kody turned to Maggie with a wicked grin. They might be getting along, but Maggie knew Kody would be trying his best to find magic that would work on her. She made a mental note to stay on her guard around him.

Maggie and her parents had their house to themselves that night after Maggie had reluctantly agreed that it would be best for her and Kody to at least maintain the illusion that Buchanan was winning. She wouldn't put it past Buchanan to carry out his threats against Kody's mom, and having Kody there at the house with her would be blatant disregard for their safety.

As soon as everyone left, Maggie felt the tension inside her growing again. She got more nervous as the evening wore on, although she didn't know why she should feel that way. Was there some event in the near future that she could somehow sense? Maggie discarded that idea quickly. She was manifesting multiple Talents, but none of them were Reader abilities. Eventually she decided that it was just the stress of everything going on, and she knew it would get worse before it got better.

Before she went to bed, Maggie tiptoed to her window and peeked out. There was no mysterious watcher there. She felt a little disappointed.

Sleep did nothing to curb Maggie's growing anxiety. When she woke up on Tuesday morning, after a fitful night, the two jewelry boxes and several framed photos on top of her dresser had been knocked to the floor. Instantly alert, Maggie began looking for other signs of an intruder. When she found none, Maggie realized she must have done it in her sleep, releasing another pulse of magic that pushed her things off the dresser.

Now Maggie could feel the magic force around her body, just as she had on Sunday. She was quiet all through breakfast and the ride to school as she focused on calming down, but her continued worry only increased the magic. At some point, Maggie knew, it would snap like a stretched rubber band, and she would inadvertently do damage to something or someone.

The walk to homeroom was a struggle, and Maggie moved slowly, trying to avoid any accidental contact with another student. She felt fragile, as if her magic might pop like a bubble if anyone touched her.

The tension suddenly began to lessen as Maggie neared her classroom. The vibration around her slackened. Finally, Maggie thought. I'm learning to control it.

A hand curled familiarly around Maggie's arm, forcing her to stop walking. Kody had dark circles under his eyes. "I could feel it around you as I walked up," he said, skipping a greeting.

"It's been getting worse since last night. It just started feeling better."

"Just now?"

"Yeah."

"You mean right when I walked up?" Kody looked smug.

"Good timing, I guess." Kody only responded with a raised eyebrow. "Okay, yes, you made me feel calmer yesterday when we were walking into school. And when you looked at me after you dropped me off at homeroom. And when I took you to the park after the battle."

"Even then?" Kody sounded surprised. "I was almost dead."

"Even then. While we were there, it was the first time I felt calm all day. And I was able to actually focus my magic and use it intentionally." Maggie stopped, recalling everything that had occurred over the previous few weeks. "In fact, I'm terrible at magic when you're not around. All of the really strong magic I've done, even if it wasn't on purpose, has been when I'm with you. Except for the nosebleed I gave Ben, but that was because I was upset."

Kody looked even more self-satisfied. "So you're

saying that me being around helps you calm down and focus, and it makes you more powerful." He laughed. "You need me. Who would have expected that?"

"Definitely not me."

A bell sounded, warning that the final bell for homeroom would be in two minutes. Kody's tone turned serious. "I have to get to class. Will you be okay?"

"Can't you give me some of this calm vibe to go?" Maggie joked.

Kody put his hand on Maggie's arm again and closed his eyes, bowing his head in concentration. He was, she knew, trying to transfer the feeling like he transferred thoughts into others. A warmth began to spread from where Kody's hand rested on her arm up into her shoulder and then down through her chest. Maggie instantly thought of drinking hot chocolate on a cold night, feeling the warmth trickle down her throat. It was comforting, enveloping. Maggie closed her eyes, too. Her head tipped forward, her forehead coming to a rest against Kody's. She could smell him, a soft mixture of soap and cologne.

The one-minute bell jolted Maggie out of the moment, and she raised her head. "Thank you," she whispered.

"See you at lunch." Kody gave her arm one last squeeze and left, leaving Maggie fighting to hold onto the feeling of tranquility that he had given her.

Maggie was on auto-pilot all morning, feeling even more distracted than she had the day before, but at least she was confident that she was in no danger of accidentally unleashing her magic. She spent most of Readers musing over the fact that Kody could affect her magically, and that it was something he had been doing unconsciously up until that morning, just as her initial magical manifestations had been unconscious.

Being immune to demon magic had prevented Kody from being able to stun her or plant thoughts in her head, so repelling those hadn't been magic on Maggie's part. What had been magic was when she burned him with her hand. It was the first time she had ever done magic. Maggie held her hand in front of her face and waggled her fingers. The binding spell her parents had put on her had lasted a lot longer than it was supposed to, but it must have started wearing off before she went to see Healer Waltham. Still, Maggie was cognizant that her first magical manifestation had happened with Kody. It was, Maggie was certain, related to him being a prophecy, but it didn't explain why Buchanan wanted to separate them. If Kody made Maggie stronger, then it would make more sense that Buchanan would want the two of them together.

All of the thoughts and possibilities made Maggie's brain feel like it was buzzing, and she was eager to discuss all of it with Kody during lunch. Maybe he would have some insight. When the bell rang at the end of Readers, Maggie rushed out, moving so quickly that she even beat Bree and Shana to their lunch table. She waited expectantly, tapping her fingers on the table. The rest of the patio filled up with students, but there was still no Bree and Shana. Kody hadn't turned up, either, and Maggie wondered if they had gone to the library instead. Feeling the first tinge of worry since that morning, Maggie gathered her backpack and went to the library, but only a handful of freshmen were inside. Her worry increased, and she walked out, looking up and down the sidewalk, not sure where to go next.

Uncertain, Maggie headed toward the lockers. It was unlikely they would be there, but she didn't know where Bree and Shana could have gone. Her route took her near the path to the student parking lot, and Maggie breathed a sigh of relief when she saw Kody walking toward her from that direction.

Instead of walking to meet her, Kody caught Maggie's eye, gestured for her to follow, and turned back around. He was walking so quickly that Maggie had to jog to catch up to him. Kody finally stopped and turned to her when they reached his car, and his expression instantly filled Maggie with dread. She somehow knew she was right as she asked, "It's about Bree and Shana, isn't it?"

"Buchanan has them. He doesn't care how he gets you on his side."

Maggie put a hand out and steadied herself against Kody. She felt sick. It's my fault, was all she could think. My fault, my fault, my fault.

Kody allowed Maggie to recover for a few moments before he added, "We can get Bree and Shana back, but it won't be easy."

"You know how to get them back?" Maggie could hear the tremor in her own voice. She wondered how panicked she would be if she had heard this news from anyone but Kody.

"Sort of." Kody looked past Maggie and pointed. "She's going to tell us."

Maggie whirled around and saw Healer Waltham. She looked troubled, and Maggie was reminded of the look on the Healer's face when she had first seen Maggie's wings.

"Why are you helping us?" Maggie said bluntly.

"Because you and your friends wouldn't be in this situation if it weren't for me." Helena sighed. "This war wouldn't be starting if it weren't for me. I should have hidden your wings the second I saw them. We could have avoided all of this." She looked at Kody, then back at Maggie. "Then again, maybe not. Some things are inevitable, like the fulfillment of prophecies."

Maggie's eyes widened. "You know the prophecy about Kody."

"So she says." Kody folded his arms over his chest. "She won't tell me."

"Because I was waiting to tell both of you at the same time. Maggie, after your call to me, I went to a demon who knows some of our most ancient lore." Helena held up one hand, palm up. "The prophecy about you ushering in the war between angels and demons is balanced by another prophecy, one known only to the demons." She held up her other hand. "The prophecy about how that war will eventually end."

"And that is?" Maggie prompted.

"The prophecy goes like this: 'The reborn Magistra Mortalis will choose as her intimate companion a boy born of a demon father. His power will destroy her and end the war.'"

CHAPTER 20

Helena   watched   Maggie   and   Kody,   their
astonishment quickly turning to denial.

Maggie was shaking her head violently. "No, Kody
makes me better. Stronger."

"I would never hurt her," Kody added emphatically.

"You say that now," Helena said. "Will you still say
the same if your own life is at risk? Will you stand by
and do nothing if the angels' victory appears eminent?"

Kody had no answer for those questions. If the
prophecy about him is true, Maggie wondered, is there
any way to alter events? Does it have to end with him
destroying me? Healer Waltham's earlier words came
back to Maggie, the warning that the prophecy could
imply danger to herself. Maggie looked over at Kody,
but he was staring down at the ground, his shoulders
slumped.

"How is it possible that the angels don't know about
Kody? Buchanan has been desperate to keep the two of
us apart." Maggie looked at Helena doubtfully.

"The prophecy was made by a demon. They knew it
was significant and something that must be kept secret.

If the Magistra Mortalis fought for the angels, then they would be over-confident. Imagine how devastating it would be for them if our half-demon destroyed their most important weapon at a crucial moment in the war. Without the Magistra Mortalis in their corner, the angels would be disorganized and, more importantly, disheartened.

"As for Buchanan," Helena continued, "he simply sees Kody's demonic blood as a threat. He figures that if you love a demon, you might fight for the demons. That's his sole motivation for wanting to separate the two of you."

Maggie was about to protest that she didn't love Kody when another thought sprang into her mind. "The demons haven't been actively recruiting me like the angels, leaving presents and stuff, because they want me fighting for the angels. They're setting me up."

"Exactly. If I had known about the second prophecy, I would have never intervened that day you met Buchanan."

Everyone, Maggie realized, wanted her to fight for the angels except for her. She still didn't want to fight for anyone. She felt resigned as she admitted that however neutral she remained, fighting was going to happen and, if the prophecy were true, it would only stop when she was dead.

I could just kill myself and stop all of this right now, Maggie thought wildly. She knew, though, that it was an option she couldn't choose. Whether it was considered self-preservation or simply selfishness, Maggie refused to give her life if there was a chance that some other course of action was possible. Besides, she had others to think of. "Tell me about Bree and Shana," Maggie said.

"I do not know where they are." Helena stopped as Maggie's expression turned critical, and she held up a hand in protest. "But I know how you can reach them. I was keeping an eye on both of you after that angel had the audacity to come onto campus yesterday. I saw the angels take your friends. You can bet they will be in Buchanan's personal care. You need to contact the angels, tell them you're willing to talk, and insist on being taken to wherever Buchanan is."

"And then what?" Maggie was incredulous. "I just demand the release of my friends and run out of there before anyone can stop me?"

"We've arranged for a little demonic distraction that should give you an advantage. Besides, you forget your power."

"I need Kody to help me control it. There is no way Buchanan will let him come with me."

"Maybe there's another way," Kody broke in. For the first time since they had heard the prophecy about him, he made eye contact with Maggie. She saw a resignation in his eyes that frightened her. "You stayed calm after I left you this morning, right? I can do it again."

Maggie didn't like anything about the situation or the plan, but she was unable to think of an alternative. She felt like she was announcing her doom when she said a simple, "Okay."

Actually getting in touch with Buchanan was the first hurdle. Maggie had no way of contacting him. It was likely that he had someone watching her every move, though. "They won't show themselves if you two are here," Maggie told Kody and Helena. "You have to go."

Kody protested, insisting that he should stay with Maggie as long as he possibly could. As she continued to refuse, Kody finally nodded his head and gave in. "Fine, but I'm going to leave you with as much power as I can spare."

"Calm and focus, too."

"Yes, and those. I'm going to try to boost your magical abilities as much as I can." Kody turned to

Helena. "Could you excuse us, please? I'd like to talk to Maggie alone before I go."

Helena smiled knowingly. "Before I go, take this, Maggie." She pulled a black velvet pouch, tied with twine, out of her pocket and handed it to Maggie.

"This is the protection bag that was on my windowsill!"

"Actually, this is a new one. You undid the magic of my first bag when you took it apart." Helena turned to Kody. "And the next time you want to go visit a girl, do it at a decent hour, not in the middle of the night." Helena winked, wished them good luck, and disappeared. Maggie chuckled softly, feeling a lot more amicable toward the Healer.

Kody took both of Maggie's hands in his own. "I don't like this," he said. "You said that I'm safer when I'm with you, but it goes both ways."

"I don't like it, either, but I don't know what else to do. I can't abandon Bree and Shana."

"Just be careful, okay?"

The earnestness in Kody's eyes made Maggie feel like her chest was tightening. In an effort to lighten the moment, she said, "I'll be fine. You're the one who's going to kill me eventually, remember?"

Kody gripped her hands tighter. "Don't say that. I would never hurt you. I'm not even sure I believe her about this secret prophecy."

"You saw the Tarot card for yourself." Maggie let out a breath. "We can't waste any more time. I'm ready when you are."

Kody closed his eyes like he had that morning, focusing his attention on transferring his magic to Maggie. She closed her eyes, as well, as the warmth began to spread from her fingers into her arms. Maggie savored the moment, knowing it was the last true peace she would feel for the foreseeable future. The warmth continued to build. Kody was pouring more into her than he had before, and soon the feeling spread through her whole body until it began to spill out, forming a layer of warmth and peace around her.

Kody's energy began to pulse, and Maggie wondered if it was in rhythm with his heartbeat or with hers. The pulsing quickened, and the warm aura along the front of Maggie's body began to grow hot. Maggie realized that Kody had moved closer to her, sending his magic not just through his hands but through his whole body. The sensation was dizzying, although she felt like her awareness of him and his magic was heightened.

A wave of heat surged through Maggie's body at the moment she felt Kody's lips against hers. Maggie eagerly kissed him back, forgetting for a moment about everything else. Kody's energy gave another pulse, stronger than before, and it rocked Maggie backwards. The kiss was broken, and Maggie knew as soon as she opened her eyes that Kody had spent almost all of his energy on her. He was breathing hard as if he had been running, and his face was drawn. Silently, Kody pulled Maggie to him and hugged her tight. "I've done as much as I can," he said. "I hope it will be enough. Find me when it's over. You know where I'll be." Kody kissed her again, softly. He climbed into his car, gave her one final look, and pulled away.

Maggie was alone, and she had no idea how she would accomplish the task ahead of her. She felt bolstered by Kody's infusion of magic. It was more than just a warmth now. The magic in her and surrounding her felt solid, like a suit of armor. Like the Knight of Swords, Maggie thought. And now I've got magic from the Knight of Wands.

Glancing around, Maggie couldn't see anyone else. She lifted her head and shouted, "Angel! I know you're watching me. Come out so you can take me to

Buchanan."

Silence was the only answer. Maggie shouted again, "I give in, okay? You guys win. Now take me to Buchanan!"

"Finally," a voice said next to her. A female had appeared beside her. She lacked the glow that angels had in their true form, and Maggie guessed it was the same woman who had posed as a grief counselor the day before. "But before we go, tell me what that demon child did to you."

"He kissed me." Maggie crossed her arms and kept her voice sarcastic. "Thanks so much for spying on that private moment."

The angel narrowed her eyes shrewdly but didn't argue. "Come on," she said. "Buchanan will be happy to see you." She grasped Maggie by the arm, and suddenly Maggie was standing in an old warehouse. Dim overhead lights showed piles of boxes and several old cars. At the center, an open area was occupied by a battered table and a chair. Buchanan sat there, studying papers, while Ajalon stood looking over his shoulder.

Maggie gasped, more surprised about seeing Ajalon alive than about the fact that she had just experienced some kind of angelic teleportation. Buchanan and Ajalon turned at the sound, and Buchanan smiled with satisfaction.

"Welcome," he said congenially. "I see we have finally found the leverage that makes you see reason."

"It's about more than Bree and Shana," Maggie said. "I've finally realized that this war begins and ends with me, and by not making a decision, I'm just delaying the inevitable." My inevitable death, Maggie added silently, though I don't know how Kody can kill me when he's not even here.

Buchanan said something quietly to Ajalon, who walked away briskly. Turning back to Maggie, he said,

"We had begun to worry that you were going to side with the demons. The incident with your friend in the first confrontation was unfortunate, of course."

Maggie held up a hand to stop Buchanan. "Don't start. You never meant to return Kody to me. You wanted him to die, and for a demon to do it. That would have gotten him out of my life and made me angry at the demons."

Buchanan started to protest, but Maggie continued, "Lying to me isn't going to accomplish anything. I want you to let my friends go, and then I'll do what I need to."

"What you witnessed a few days ago was merely a little skirmish. Do you think your power has progressed to the point that you can control a full-scale battle?"

Maggie smiled, feeling a new sense of confidence swelling inside her. "I know it has."

Buchanan began to return the smile, but his expression faltered when two angels appeared in front of him. "The demons have attacked our troops. They came out of nowhere," one said quickly. His voice shook. "They're fighting like they're on a kamikaze mission. Our troops are overwhelmed by their numbers and their ferocity."

"Ajalon!" Buchanan shouted. The angel appeared, with Bree and Shana in tow. Both girls were unharmed. Maggie's smile widened, and she waved at them as if the situation was totally normal and she was simply greeting them at their lunch table. Bree began to say something as her brows contracted in confusion, but Shana shushed her, looking at Maggie as if she knew there was more to her friend that couldn't be seen.

Ajalon shot to attention when he heard his name, and Buchanan fired off orders to him. "Bring additional troops to our encampment. The battle has begun. I'll take Maggie there myself." Ajalon gave a nod and disappeared, but not before casting a look of abhorrence at Maggie.

The demon attack was the distraction Helena had mentioned, Maggie was sure. How it was supposed to help her, though, was something Maggie was less certain about.

"I had envisioned something of a smaller exercise for your first time leading us into battle," Buchanan said to Maggie. "However, nothing like jumping in with both feet. We're about to learn just how well you can control your magic."

The two angels who had come from the battle approached. At Buchanan's command, one grasped Maggie by the shoulder and the other placed a hand on Buchanan. The scene in front of Maggie shifted, and she saw a slew of angels before her, all holding weapons and yelling as they roused themselves into a fervor for the battle. They were formidable, their wings outstretched and the glow from their skin seeming to radiate an almost painful brightness. Maggie had to squint to look at them.

They were in a small clearing in a wooded area. Maggie didn't know where they actually were, but judging by the bare trees and the colder temperature, she figured they were somewhere further north.

The angels had all fallen silent when they saw Buchanan. Now, he spread his arms wide. "God and the Magistra Mortalis are with you. Go and defeat the demons!" A cheer went up, and as one, the angels hoisted their weapons into the air. Ajalon shouted a command, and they filed out of the clearing, flying up and over the trees.

"Follow them," Buchanan was looking at Maggie intently. "You need to see the battle to properly control it."

Maggie took a few steps forward, but stopped when Buchanan barked, "Fly, of course."

As Maggie slid out of her light jacket and unfurled her wings, she asked, "And Bree and Shana?"

"Safe."

"Not good enough. I want them here, where I can see them." Buchanan huffed and nodded to a nearby angel. She disappeared and reappeared just a few seconds later, Bree and Shana in her grip. Satisfied, Maggie looked for a long time at her friends to remind herself why she was doing this before she flapped her wings and rose into the air. She heard an excited "ooh!" from Shana and had to laugh. It was the first time she and Bree had seen Maggie fly, and even in the middle of a battle and being held captive, Shana could still appreciate Maggie's skill. The unexpected reaction made Maggie's heart feel lighter, and she soared over the woods, following the direction the angels had taken.

Soon, Maggie saw them ahead of her, but they were not alone. The angels she had seen in the clearing were just a small part of the reinforcements, and it seemed to Maggie that there had to be at least a thousand of them flying through the air, grappling with just as many demons. The angel who had reported to Buchanan had not been exaggerating about the ferocity of the demons: they lunged at the angels, heedless of the risks. Many had already fallen to the ground, where even more fighting was taking place.

Maggie stopped, hovering in the air outside the fray. The scene was sickening. The angels who had been fighting since the start had red stains on their white wings and clothing. Feathers floated in the air, and Maggie had the ridiculous vision of a pillow fight gone horribly wrong. As she watched, a group of at least twenty demons appeared not far from her. They barely glanced at her as they charged into the battle.

She had led Buchanan to believe that she was there to fight for the angels, but Maggie had no intention of following through on that. She had gotten herself this far, but Bree and Shana were not yet safe, and stalling would only result in more death on both sides.

How am I supposed to pick a side? Maggie thought. The angels are using threats and deceit to get their way, and the demons are waiting to unleash Kody on me. Neither side is in the right, and I don't want to help either one.

Buchanan's previous words echoed in Maggie's head. She heard him tell her that she would choose a side, even if it was unconscious on her part. Maggie flew higher and positioned herself over the battle. The sound of the swords and spears meeting made a cacophony that hurt her ears. There was a loud scream, and Maggie saw an angel fall to the ground. The demon who had pierced him with a spear wheeled around and began to attack another angel.

Maggie felt her fear trying to overpower her, and she fought it down, picturing Kody in her mind. "I have power, and I have control," she said softly to herself. The image of Kody reminded her of her earlier response to Buchanan's declaration that she would choose a side: "I fight for Kody." Not just Kody, Maggie realized, but for herself, her friends, and everyone else she knew. "I'm fighting for the humans," she said out loud. A surge of power pulsed through her, and Maggie saw those fighting just below her swerve and dip under its force. Maggie said the words louder. It was the right choice.

Maggie felt another buildup of power, and this time, she didn't try to hold it back. A wave of magic ripped through her and down into the battle below. The angel nearest her stiffened, his wings frozen in place. He seemed to hover in mid-air for a moment, and then his body fell. Maggie watched as it plummeted, her own wings faltering as the angel's body slammed into the ground. She hadn't been sure about the fate of the warriors she had affected in the battle at her house, but she knew this angel was dead. His neck and legs were at sickening angles to the rest of his prone body.

Maggie cried out, horrified at what she had done. Her eyes remained fixed on the dead angel, but movement near her finally made her bring her head back up. Another angel, this one a woman with black demon blood spattered across her face, had flown up to Maggie.

"You're supposed to be fighting for us! You need to get your power under control!" The angel raised her sword at Maggie, the point just a few inches away from Maggie's chest.

The guilt that Maggie felt was swiftly replaced by anger. "My power *is* under control," Maggie said quietly. The angel faltered, her sword dipping slightly as she detected the malice in Maggie's voice.

The next time Maggie spoke, it was a shout. To her ears, it seemed as if her voice was amplified, and she felt rather than saw the hundreds of angels and demons who turned to stare at her. "I fight for the humans!"

The angel reared back, but her look of hesitation transformed into rage. She flapped her wings a few times, hovering, then launched herself at Maggie, her sword now aimed at Maggie's heart.

With no time to think, Maggie let her instincts take over. Whether it was her human instinct for survival or battle instincts from her Magistra Mortalis blood, she didn't know. Maggie's wings ceased beating and she dropped five feet. At the same time, she raised her hand, sending a concentrated wave of magic toward the attacking angel. The angel's body rocked backward.

Maggie flapped her wings harder, regaining the altitude she had lost just as the angel completed a graceful backflip to float in front of Maggie once again. For a second time, the angel lunged. Maggie barely avoided the sword as she swerved right, and suddenly

Maggie felt like she was watching a movie on fast-forward. The angel attacked again and again, and each time Maggie was nearly one step behind. The sword grazed her shoulder one time, drawing a thin line of blood. Maggie realized that if she continued to simply defend herself, the angel would eventually overwhelm her.

The next time the angel sped forward, Maggie whirled around so that she was behind the angel. Quickly, she put her hand on the angel's back, trying to send thoughts of surrender into the angel's mind.

Without enough time to really concentrate, though, Maggie's attempt was futile. The angel began to turn, and Maggie sent out another wave of magic. Her hand was still pressed to the angel's back, and the power was released directly into her body. The angel convulsed as she looked at Maggie with surprise. If the fight had been on fast-forward before, then now it was in slow motion as the angel's eyes unfocused and her face went slack. Just as her body began to fall, Maggie reached down and took the sword from her limp hand.

Maggie's breath came in shuddering gasps. She had killed two angels. She tried to calm down, reminding herself that she would now be dead if she hadn't fought back, but she felt nauseated at what she had done. Before she could recover, another angel swooped toward Maggie, his shout incoherent as he brought the point of his spear up for an attack.

Maggie gripped the sword and was again surprised at how confident she felt with such a weapon in her hand. In her mind she saw the Knight of Swords, a sword in one hand and a wand in the other. Healer Waltham had warned her that Kody would be incredibly powerful, but armed for war and filled with magic, Maggie knew that she was more powerful than even Buchanan could have imagined. That thought gave her courage, and Maggie brought the sword up to parry the angel's spear thrust. Undaunted, the angel continued to strike. He and Maggie flew in circles, both of them focused solely on the other.

Neither one of them saw the demon that flew up beneath them. With a deft slash of his knife, he opened a gash on the angel's lower leg. The angel howled in pain. Caught off guard, Maggie paused, unsure whether to protect herself from the angel or the demon.

She needed to protect herself from both. They rounded on her, and suddenly Maggie was parrying the angel's spear with her sword while darting through the sky in an effort to avoid the demon's knife slashes.

Maggie screamed when the knife finally found a mark, tearing into her thigh. The demon laughed, a manic sound that made Maggie shudder. She slashed down violently with her sword, wanting to stop the laughter as much as she wanted to defend herself. Her sword caught the demon in the chest, the blade sinking into the skin over his heart. The laugh cut off with a choking sound before the demon fell, dead, to the ground below.

With the demon out of the fight, Maggie was able to turn her attention back to the angel, only to find two more angels hovering next to him. Maggie raised her sword just as four demons materialized next to her. They attacked the angels, ignoring Maggie completely. "Where is our own prophecy?" she heard one demon shout. "Where is our victory?"

Maggie glanced around her, but the other warriors near her were too engaged in their own battles to notice her. She flew higher. As she rose, the angel she had been fighting impaled a demon with his spear, then turned his gaze to her. Maggie shook her head, realizing that the angel wouldn't stop until one of them was dead.

The angel raised his spear, but Maggie brought her sword up hard, snapping the shaft in two before its tip could pierce her. She used the momentum to arc the sword back down, the blade hitting the angel in the neck. A spray of blood colored the air red as the angel's body tumbled downward.

Maggie felt a surge in her stomach and thought she was going to be sick. Instead, she grasped the sword tightly and focused on the feel of the smooth grip under her palm. The weight of the weapon was reassuring. Watching the violence that continued below her, Maggie felt even more confident that she had made the right decision by siding with the human race. The Earth was no place for a war between the higher beings.

The feeling that she was right did nothing to help Maggie decide on a course of action. She wasn't willing to simply destroy everyone below her in the battle. Even if she did, there would be more troops from each side, and the destruction wouldn't end until both the angels and the demons were wiped out. Or, Maggie realized, until Kody wiped her out. She had believed him when he said he would never hurt her, but what if the demons took his mom hostage and forced Kody to make a choice between her or them? Maggie resolved that she would never let it come to that.

The battle raged on, and soldiers on each side continued to plummet to the earth, injured or dead, and still Maggie hovered above them, frozen in her indecision. Her thoughts crept back to the idea of killing herself, knowing the war would come to a halt with her death. She considered flying down into the midst of the battle, throwing herself into the path of a sword. Maggie grimaced at the idea of the pain that would bring. Then she thought of the magic that Kody had imbued her with, and she wondered if she could simply destroy herself. Maggie gasped as a realization struck. If she used magic to kill herself, then it would be with not just her magic, but with Kody's, as well. Even without him present, he could inadvertently fulfill the prophecy about him.

Death was still not the option Maggie wanted to consider. If only she could make herself useless to the angels and the demons, they would have no help in the war. If she could make herself not be a Magistra Mortalis anymore, they would stop fighting and leave her alone. And, Maggie hoped, free Bree and Shana.

Maggie thought hard. How could she do that? Putting a binding spell on herself, like her parents had done when she was a child, only hid her abilities. She needed to get rid of them altogether. She reasoned that if she and Kody had been able to put thoughts in people's minds, then it was possible to make people forget. It wouldn't be an easy task, Maggie knew, to make herself forget her magic. She would have to wipe out an innate ability, not just a memory.

I'll be a No Talent again, Maggie thought wistfully.

Maggie flew down, skirting the battle and landing on the ground. She whispered, "Oblitus alae," and her wings disappeared. Suddenly, the fierce-looking Magistra Mortalis who had been overseeing the battle seemed very small and afraid. Maggie wasn't even certain that she could remove her magical abilities, but the idea of it being the fulfillment of the prophecy about Kody gave her hope that it might work.

There was a rustle behind Maggie, and she turned to see Buchanan. He had flown out to observe the battle, and now he loomed over Maggie, his wings giving him even more of an impressive presence. "What are you doing?" Buchanan's face was red.

"Very powerful magic." Maggie could hear the temerity in her voice.

"Then what are you waiting for? My troops are getting slaughtered up there!"

"Then I suggest you leave me alone."

Buchanan crossed his arms and stood firm, clearly

suspicious of Maggie. With a shrug, she closed her eyes and tried to block out the feeling of Buchanan standing so close to her. She thought of Kody transferring his magic to her. Magic and control. In her mind, Maggie saw that magic merging with her own, combined forces that grew bright inside her.

How can I destroy my magic if I'm using my magic to do it? Maggie shook her head, as if she could sling the thought out of her mind. I'll use my magic, she told herself, until I don't have it anymore.

She focused harder, and the mental image darkened and became black, a void that would obliterate anything it met. Maggie felt its power increase, a concentrated mass of annihilation, and she sent it deep into her brain, concentrating on her abilities as a Magistra Mortalis. A pressure began to grow inside her skull, and Maggie dropped her sword, clutching her hands to her head. Still, she continued to focus. A noise crept into Maggie's awareness, like the faraway sound of a siren. Maggie's own voice, wailing. There was a sudden stab of pain in her head, and then a blow to her side, and Maggie fell to the ground as a last, powerful pulse of magic exploded from her body.

Buchanan was standing over Maggie when she opened her eyes. He had her sword in his hand, and its tip was stained anew with bright red blood. From the wetness she felt on her right side, Maggie knew it was hers. Buchanan had realized that whatever Maggie was doing, it wasn't in the best interest of the angels, and he had tried to break her concentration by hurting her.

Maggie felt a dullness inside her. The pulsing power she had felt before, the warm glow of Kody's magic, all of it was gone. She was tired and weak, and she knew that the magic had worked against itself. She was back to being normal, a No Talent who would be ostracized at school and forced to watch as her friends used abilities she would never again experience.

Buchanan took a deep breath and opened his mouth to shout, but before he could form words, a demon appeared in front of Maggie. Her right cheek had been slashed, and dark blood oozed down her face. "She's here!" the demon shouted.

A second demon, a male, appeared next to the first, and Maggie cried out when she saw Kody standing stiffly next to him, a knife held against his side. Despite the danger of the situation, Kody looked at Maggie sheepishly. "I should have known they would drag me into it," he said.

"Shut up!" the demon holding Kody hissed. He jerked his chin in Maggie's direction. "Destroy her, Prophecy!"

Kody winced as the knife tip pierced his side, but his eyes blazed. "No," he said simply.

"What is going on?" Buchanan's anger had been replaced by confusion, and he took a step backward.

"You'll find out as soon as the child fulfills his prophecy," the female demon said.

"It's too late," Maggie said. "The prophecy has been fulfilled already."

"Impossible!" the demon said at the same time that Kody said, "But you're still alive!"

"What is going on?" Buchanan roared the question this time. He still stood over Maggie, his body shaking in a mixture of rage and horror. "What have you done?"

"I've ended the war. I can't help anyone anymore." Maggie felt tears sliding down her cheeks as she gingerly stood. "My magic is gone."

"You deceitful bitch!" Buchanan raged. "You said you would help us!" He raised the sword, but before he could strike a blow, he stiffened, dropping the sword as his eyes widened in surprise. When he turned around, Maggie saw a thin tree branch sticking out of the skin under his left wing. She followed Buchanan's line of sight and saw Shana, hands raised toward him. Another branch was already hovering in front of her, ready to fly. Bree stood next to her, her hands curled into fists.

The two demons yelped in celebration. The male demon instantly released Kody and flew upwards, repeating, "The prophecy is fulfilled!" The demons who heard the words attacked the angels with renewed vigor, convinced that they were going to end the war in a swift victory.

Without a word, Buchanan reached back and plucked the stick from his body. He took several deep breaths before he shouted, "Destroy the Magistra Mortalis and her friends!"

A dozen angels who managed to elude the demons alighted on the ground near Maggie and her friends, heeding Buchanan's call. Kody rushed to Maggie's side and stood shoulder-to-shoulder with her. Behind them, Bree and Shana were facing the opposite direction, the four of them forming a tight circle.

Maggie scooped up her sword, and several drops of her own blood dripped from its tip. The image of the Tarot cards popped into her mind again, both her and Kody armed with a sword and a wand. Kody had given Maggie his magic to make her both a warrior and a powerful magic user, completing the scene for the Knight of Swords. By that logic, Maggie figured, it was up to her to complete the scene for the Knight of Wands.

The angels began to advance slowly. Some of them were smiling maliciously.

What should I do? Maggie thought wildly. I've destroyed my magic, so how can I help Kody?

Maggie raised her sword, and she suddenly knew that the answer was so simple. She handed the sword to Kody. "You have to fight this battle, but you'll win," she said firmly. "I chose us to win, not the angels or the demons. You gave me your magic, and I've given you the victory."

Wordlessly, Kody accepted the sword. He took a breath, squeezed Maggie's hand, then turned to the angels. With a cry, he lifted the sword over his head with both hands and rushed forward.

The angels had been focused on Maggie, and they were caught off guard by Kody's sudden attack. Several angels fought him, but Kody never relinquished control of the battle. Maggie had filled him with confidence, and his fearless fighting made the angels hesitate. Kody caught one in the side, then deftly brought the sword around to block the blows from another. He began moving away from Maggie, drawing the attention of the angels away from her.

Maggie bent and picked up a spear that one of the angels had dropped. She tried to fend off the two angels who were rushing toward her, but the blood loss from the wound in her side was making her lightheaded. Her vision blurred slightly, and she felt her arm falter.

Suddenly, the spear wrenched itself out of Maggie's grip and shot forward, its tip sinking into the forehead of the closest angel. The other angel tripped and fell forward, hitting the ground hard. Bree appeared behind him briefly, her invisibility giving her a distinct advantage as she darted in and out of view.

Maggie glanced around and saw that Kody had left a path of dead angels in his wake. He whirled around an angel who was advancing, avoiding the attack to run away from the battle. Surprised, Maggie looked in the direction that Kody was running and saw Buchanan, who was hustling toward the woods as quickly as he could.

Kody caught Buchanan while they were still on open ground, moving in front of him and raising the sword so that its tip rested against Buchanan's chest. Maggie couldn't hear what Kody said to him, but Buchanan bowed his head and his shoulders slumped.

Slowly, Buchanan turned and faced the battlefield. "Enough! The war is over!" Buchanan announced.

The angels slowly, reluctantly, stopped their assault on Maggie, Bree and Shana. Maggie walked toward Buchanan, limping from the knife wound in her thigh. She reached Buchanan just as the demon who had brought Kody to the battle flew down.

"You surrender?" the demon asked, grinning.

"Not to you," Buchanan said. "To her. Neither angels nor demons will have dominion over this Earth. She chose humankind." Buchanan pronounced the word with disgust.

The demon's grin turned into a sneer as he rounded on Maggie. Then, unexpectedly, he laughed. "Free will," he said. "I admire your style, Magistra Mortalis." Without waiting for Maggie to respond, the demon flew back into the battle to spread the word.

Buchanan glared at Maggie. "You don't have your powers or the prophecy to protect you now," he said menacingly. How quickly he went from defeated to vengeful, Maggie thought. "You have won this war, but this is far from the last fight for you."

As Buchanan walked away, Shana stepped up to Maggie's side. "I'm going to tell my mom not to watch his show anymore."

The battle broke up quickly. Angels and demons flew to the ground, grabbed their dead and wounded, and disappeared. Within a minute, the battlefield was empty except for Maggie, Kody, Bree and Shana. As the adrenaline faded from her veins, Maggie slid to the ground.

Bree fell to her knees next to Maggie and began examining the wound on her side. "Are you okay? No, of course you're not." Bree pulled off her hoodie and pressed it against Maggie's side. "We need to get you to a hospital."

"We don't even know where we are."

"We're somewhere around Richmond, Virginia," Shana spoke up. She had her back to the others, keeping a watchful eye on the battlefield in case anyone came back. "I heard one of the angels mention it."

"But which direction should we even go? We have no idea where a road might be." Bree tied the ends of her hoodie around Maggie's waist in a makeshift bandage and stood, searching for some sign of civilization.

Maggie got to her feet carefully with Kody's help. The pain in her side was acute, but she didn't think Buchanan had stabbed her too deeply. "I lost my magic, but I might still have my wings. Manifestum alae!" To her great relief, Maggie's wings appeared. She pumped her fist, then winced. "This is going to hurt."

"Stop," Kody said. "Let me." He looked exhausted after his magical and physical exertions, but he handed the sword to Maggie, manifested his wings and flew up over the battlefield. Looking across the horizon, he spied a road and, even better, a gas station just a mile or two away. Kody pointed, looking down to make sure Maggie saw the direction he was indicating.

Once he was back on the ground, Kody hid his wings while Maggie did the same. He put a steadying arm around her as they began moving slowly toward the road.

"You were brilliant," Maggie said.

"Thanks to you. It's nice having you on my side."

"But I can't help you anymore. Besides, it's over."

"I don't think it is," Kody muttered, thinking of Buchanan. He glanced down at the sword, still tight in Maggie's hand. She carried it almost unconsciously, as if she was used to having it in her grip. She sagged against Kody as they walked, but the arm holding the sword seemed to have a life and energy of its own. Kody smiled grimly, and his voice was confident when he spoke again. "And when he comes for us, we'll be ready."

Epilogue

"How did it feel to ace your senior Physicals test today?" Kody asked. He and Maggie were sitting on the back steps of the cabin, snuggled under a blanket that Kody had retrieved from inside.

"You know exactly how it feels," Maggie said. "You aced the test, too. It does feel nice to finally be good in a Talents class." Maggie had loved the chance to show off her flying abilities in front of her classmates. She and Kody had been immediately transferred to the class once Maggie had recovered from her injuries, and she had enjoyed school more in the past few weeks than she had in years. The taunting had stopped, and while some kids still looked nervously at her, most had already moved on to more current gossip.

"If I can't be the hero of the demons, I may as well be the hero of Physicals class," Kody said wryly.

"I don't want to be a hero to anybody." Maggie nestled closer against Kody. "I'm just fine being plain old me."

"Says the girl with red wings." Kody leaned in and kissed Maggie. Abruptly, he pulled back. "I'm not doing that," he said, nodding toward the porch lights. They were blinking off and on rhythmically.

Maggie smiled. "I guess I didn't destroy quite all of my magic."

ABOUT THE AUTHOR

Beth Dolgner started writing short stories at a young age, and having a journalism teacher for a dad certainly set her on the right track. *Georgia Spirits and Specters*, Beth's first book, debuted in the spring of 2009 and was followed by *Everyday Voodoo* in 2010. Beth made her fiction debut in 2011 with the paranormal romance *Ghost of a Threat*, the first in the Betty Boo, Ghost Hunter series. In her free time, Beth enjoys traveling, sewing and costuming. She and her husband Ed live in Atlanta, Georgia, with their four cats.

Nonfiction books by Beth Dolgner
Everyday Voodoo
Georgia Spirits and Specters

The Betty Boo, Ghost Hunter Series
Ghost of a Threat
Ghost of a Whisper
Ghost of a Memory
Ghost of a Hope

Manifest, An Alice Meriwether Novel

For more information, visit bethdolgner.com.

www.ingramcontent.com/pod-product-compliance
Lightning Source LLC
Chambersburg PA
CBHW020618180626
46810CB00007B/2828